Can Kelly dare let herself fall in love with Steven, a skydiver, a man so different from herself?

His eyes opened, and he looked at her with a smile. "It surprises you that I'm not an uncultured lout? You've enjoyed thinking of me that way, haven't you?"

"You never contradicted me," she countered.

He laughed gently, the sound too light to disturb the quiet of their mood. "I played a game; I often do, you know. It amused me to let you think the worst of me."

"And now?"

"And now I want to play a different role. I don't want you to see me as the. . .daredevil I sometimes pretend to be."

"Must you always pretend?" Kelly asked.

"I'm not now."

Kelly didn't dare look at him, for the tension that had momentarily abated in her delight at the wonders of the sky now returned in full force. Every muscle seemed suddenly vibrant and alive, tingling with sensation.

She heard him move and flashed a look at him, affirming what she suspected: he was raised on one elbow, staring into her face, only inches away. Her voice choked and she could only say hoarsely, "Steven, no."

PHYLLIS HUMPHREY makes her home in California. *Flying High* marks her debut with **Heartsong Presents.**

Flying
High

Phyllis Humphrey

Heartsong Presents

A note from the Author:
I love to hear from my readers! You may write to me at
the following address: **Phyllis Humphrey**
Author Relations
P.O. Box 719
Uhrichsville, OH 44683

ISBN 1-55748-767-7

FLYING HIGH

Cover illustration by Gary Maria.

PRINTED IN THE U.S.A.

one

Kelly Marsh hugged her sweater tightly around her slim figure to ward off the chill of the early morning air. As she watched, a small airplane, a Cessna 150, taxied down the middle of the street, then stopped before turning into the parking lot of the shopping center.

"Here it comes!" Her hired photographer called the words to her over his shoulder, then ran alongside the slowly moving aircraft, snapping publicity pictures. The gradually clearing sky revealed other vehicles behind, and Kelly, her long blond hair lifted above her neck by a slight breeze, wondered who had joined the procession, for few cars could be expected to come to the shopping center at this hour of the morning.

Two motorcycles, their engines drowning out other sounds, roared ahead, then stopped just inside the lot. Kelly strode toward them.

"You Miss Marsh?" one of the uniformed policemen asked, removing his helmet and gloves.

"Yes, thanks for your help."

"You're welcome, ma'am. We've never had to escort an airplane taxiing down a street before, but there were no problems. There's two more motorcycles bringing up the rear, and between us, we managed to keep things under control."

"It must have been quite a sight to the early-morning commuters: seeing a plane on the highway."

"There could have been problems," the officer admitted,

"if some people let this distract them from their driving."

Kelly shivered slightly at the thought. What if some sleepy-eyed motorist on his way to work—or coming home from a swing-shift job—had seen this apparition and panicked, crashing into another car or the center divider? She thanked God such a thing hadn't happened.

"But fortunately," the officer continued, "the airport isn't too far, and we only had to be on the streets for a few miles. If you do this more often," he added, with a smile, "perhaps you'd better think about building an airport on the edge of the shopping center!"

Kelly smiled back. "I don't even work for the shopping center, much less own it. I'm just running the promotion here. However, I doubt that I'll ever try moving an airplane on the streets again."

The officer replaced his helmet, and he and his partner wheeled their bikes back to the street and departed with a roar of engines.

Turning toward the small plane, Kelly noticed it heading straight for her, its destination seemingly the very spot on which she stood. Scarcely five feet in front of her, it stopped, the door opened, and a man stepped out in front of her.

Although his deeply-tanned face seemed at least ten inches above her own, she saw closely-cropped, black, curly hair and features that were finely chiseled, giving him an aristocratic appearance, one that seemed completely out of character with the blue jumpsuit stretched taut over his broad shoulders.

"Well, hello..." he drawled, his voice deep and rich. Before she could answer, he thrust his hand forward and caught hers, pressing firmly. It was large and warm, and hers seemed lost in it. She realized, as he opened his eyes wider, that they were startlingly blue under thick dark lashes.

"How do you do? I'm Kelly Marsh, from Ingersoll Productions." The words came automatically, in spite of the fact that his touch and his look were affecting her strangely. Never before had she felt imprisoned by a man's look, mesmerized by his stare. Seconds seemed to turn into hours.

Pulling her hand from his, she concentrated her gaze on the patch over the left breast pocket of his jumpsuit.

"Steven Barry," the man said. "I'm delivering this plane to your boss."

"To my boss?" His words startled her into looking up at his face again. "I'm the...that is, I mean, I'm in charge here."

"You're in charge?" He paused and his thorough appraisal of her left her somewhat unsettled. He looked at her as if calmly determining her height and weight and whether he would like to push her aside like a fly, or crush her to him in an embrace. "You're just a girl," he said finally. "You can't be in charge."

Kelly supposed her long hair blowing freely and the fact that she wore pants today instead of her usual tailored suit and high heels, made her appear young. But, in fact, she was almost twenty-five. "I'm in charge, nevertheless," she said, ignoring his obviously chauvinistic attitude.

Her green eyes sparkled, and rosy spots of color bloomed in her cheeks, as she realized Mr. Steven Barry was voicing her own original feelings about this particular job. She remembered how she had pleaded not to be given the assignment, but Lyle Durning, her new boss, brooked no arguments. He had been regional director of promotions for only a month, yet so eager to plunge in, even before he learned the business, that he had chosen Kelly, of all people, to handle this promotion. She had tactfully pointed out to him that there were others more qualified than she, but he countered that by saying one of his tasks as new division manager included being certain that any person in the company could handle any kind of assignment. There seemed to be an additional hint in his voice that if she didn't want to cooperate, he could find someone to take her place permanently.

"Besides," she told Steven Barry, bringing her thoughts back to the present, "you're not Mr. Johnson. I made the arrangements with him."

"So you did," he said, visibly relaxing. "I shouldn't have spoken as I did. I am *not* in charge today, only the chauffeur. I thought I shouldn't miss a chance to taxi a plane on the street instead of a runway."

"Then you're a pilot," Kelly asked, looking over his jumpsuit once more.

"Yes, I am. Mainly, however, I'm the resident skydiving instructor. That's what I prefer to do."

Kelly knew even less about skydiving than she did about piloting planes, but she knew she never could have imagined a more dangerous and ridiculous sport. How could anyone claim to like risking his life in such an absurd way?

But before she could reply to him, a car, headlights piercing the gloom, came from behind the airplane and caught Kelly's attention. When it stopped, a slender, middle-aged man, his red hair mixed with gray, climbed out.

"Good morning," he said. "I'm Red Johnson. We spoke on the phone."

"Kelly Marsh. I can see where you get your nickname," she said, smiling and shaking his outstretched hand. "I had thought you'd be in the airplane, but I see you had someone else. . .er, drive it."

"One of the best, Steven Barry," he answered. "He's—"

Steven stopped him with a look, and Kelly wondered

what the younger man did not want Johnson to say. In the brief moments of their conversation, she had already determined that Steven Barry, although certainly handsome, was the type of man she had been avoiding all her life: chauvinistic and no doubt arrogant and conceited as well.

They were joined then by a plump, fortyish-looking man whom Kelly recognized as Ed Kozinsky, the maintenance manager of the shopping center.

"Good morning, Mr. Kozinsky," she said. "Thanks for coming so early." She introduced everyone and then asked Kozinsky, "Is everything ready for the plane to come onto the mall?"

"Yes," he answered, rubbing a hand over his balding head. "I think we can bring it in between buildings J and H, as we planned."

"Fine," Kelly said. "I'll leave it in your hands then."

Feeling she was not needed at the moment, and that she ought to check on other parts of the center, Kelly nodded to the men and walked rapidly to the sidewalk that ran between the two nearest buildings. The concrete widened and became a broad mall, dotted here and there with large stone planters holding trees, shrubs, and flowers. She had shopped here many times, since she lived in an apartment close by, but now she looked at it not as a shopper but as a promoter, visualizing where the various exhibits would be placed.

Walking quickly, she went all the way to the south end of the center, and noticed with satisfaction that the wooden ramps were already in place so that the trailers carrying boats and mobile homes could get over the curb. Turning around and going in the opposite direction, almost a full city block, she checked the north entrance as well. That, too, appeared ready for the exhibits. On the west, there were only narrow entrances from the parking lot to the main mall, so that only small displays could enter from that direction. Finally, having spent half an hour on her tour, she headed back to the eastern side again. The plane would be appearing here any moment. She glanced at her watch. It was half past five.

She looked up toward the brightening sky above the distant hills. Soon the heat of summer would settle into this valley and force her to shed her sweater or head for her air conditioned office.

Kelly liked the heat, loved the sun which had already bleached her golden hair even lighter, though it was only June, just as she loved this part of California. The broad San Joaquin valley was not the most populated part of the state, but that only added to its appeal for her. She liked the open spaces, fertile farms and more identifiable seasons—hot, dry days in summer and cool wet ones in winter. Besides, it wasn't far to the denser, better known regions of California. In four hours she could be visiting her widowed mother in Pasadena, close to Los Angeles, where she had grown up. Similarly, only four hours driving in a northerly direction would take her to San Francisco, to enjoy the charm of the city set on hills, its spectacular Golden Gate Bridge, crooked streets, and clanging cable cars.

As she rounded a small kiosk built into the center of the mall, a figure loomed in front of her, interrupting her reverie. She backed up involuntarily. It was the skydiver, Steven Barry.

"Oh," she said. "You frightened me."

"Do you frighten easily?" he asked, his tone inquisitive.

"No, of course not. It's just that I wasn't expecting anyone else to be here."

As if he weren't listening, he suddenly stooped down to the planter nearby and snapped off a blossom from the flower bed. The pansy's bright yellow petals surrounded a deep purple center, and dew clung to it.

"Here," he said, coming close and pushing the stem between strands of yarn on the shoulder of her sweater. "It suits you." Kelly backed away further, disturbed by his aggressive demeanor. "You shouldn't have—"

"I often do things I shouldn't. Life is more fun that way."

"Taking things is fun?" As soon as she said the words, she regretted them. She felt intimidated by the man for some reason and found herself saying the first thing that came to mind. Taking the flower was a trivial matter, not worth mentioning. Why did he have such an effect on her?

"Are you one of those uptight people?" he demanded, and the piercing blue eyes he turned on her again unnerved her.

She glanced at the flower's bright splash of color on her white sweater and wondered how to reply. He seemed to be deliberately baiting her, and the temptation came to reply in kind, but she resisted.

"I don't think I'm being uptight. However—"

"The flowers are there for enjoyment, aren't they?" he interrupted. "Well, I enjoy them more this way. The color exactly matches the color of your hair, like spun gold."

She couldn't think of an answer. What a maddening creature he was: first mocking, then critical, and now flattering.

"Thank you," she said, and her voice sounded high and thin in her ears, like a schoolgirl being complimented by the teacher for a good term paper.

"You're quite beautiful, you know," he said then.

Kelly's discomfort increased. She had heard similar

things several times in her life, and although she enjoyed the compliments, she never believed she was beautiful. Her mouth was too wide and her nose the tiniest bit crooked. Not that it mattered; she tried never to be vain.

She managed to find her voice and look up at him, hoping to keep her face composed. "Do you always talk this way to complete strangers?"

"I never say anything that isn't true."

"Well, thank you very much, but I'd rather not discuss myself. I'd better get back." She attempted to go around him, to resume her walk back to the east entrance, but he put his hands on her shoulders and held her still.

"I want to ask you a question."

"Yes?" she asked, aware of his strong touch and a masculine scent that clung to him.

"Here, let's sit down." He swung her about and led her to a wooden bench set into the side of a planter. "I haven't figured out just why you're in charge here."

His tone said he felt he had the right to know everything, and Kelly struggled with the antagonism she felt. She was usually able to handle such people, but this one was a real challenge.

"I understand your interest," she said, keeping her voice low and gentle, "but both Flyway Aviation and Ingersoll Productions seem satisfied that I'm the right person." She smiled. "I made the arrangements with Mr. Johnson, and as you admitted earlier, you just came along this morning to drive the airplane up the highway."

"Red told me he made arrangements with Ingersoll, not with some pretty girl."

His continuing compliments didn't help Kelly's mood. "The way I look has nothing to do with my job. I'm a public relations director for Ingersoll and I'm in charge of this sports promotion. And I wish, Mr. Barry, that you wouldn't alternately flatter and insult me."

She tried to rise, but he had only to put one hand on her forearm, and she found herself seated again.

"Please call me Steven," he said. "And I didn't mean to insult you. I always thought it complimentary for a woman to be considered beautiful."

"I appreciate your motives, but women today don't like to be called 'girls,' and—"

"Right," he interrupted. "Saying a woman is beautiful these days amounts to sexual harassment."

"I'm not accusing you of harassment," Kelly said. This time she succeeded in rising because he didn't attempt to restrain her. "But I'm no longer a girl. It so happens I have a college degree and years of experience." She emphasized "years," but in fact, her experience consisted of exactly two.

She felt pleased with her answer, but he rose also, and towering over her as he did, she found herself feeling less than commanding.

"Okay, I'm sorry," he said. "I just thought—"

"You thought I shouldn't be in charge of getting an airplane onto this mall." Once more Kelly expressed silent gratitude that the morning's adventure had not included an accident. Then she would not only have lost her job for certain, with small consolation in the knowledge that she had told her boss she didn't want to handle this particular promotion in the first place, but the thought of causing an accident would have haunted her the rest of her days.

"One airplane, yes," Steven affirmed. "But in addition—the newspaper said—you'll have four sailboats, six power boats, three motor homes, and a complete log cabin on this mall today, not to mention tents, camp stoves, tennis racquets, skis—"

"I know about the newspaper article," Kelly said, impressed that he could quote all the details. "I wrote the story myself."

"Did you?" He smiled at her. "But as for running this thing, I expected some muscle-bound athlete, not—and forgive me if I'm again skirting the edge of politically correct conversation—a young woman who looks as if she should be sitting in a flower garden listening to music and doing needlepoint."

This Steven Barry was obviously no muscle-bound athlete himself, even if he did include flying and skydiving among his pursuits. Furthermore, he was so right about her. She had said almost the same things to her boss only three weeks ago. A liberal arts graduate, she had studied literature, art, music, drama, history. Her previous assignments, since joining the public relations firm, had been art showings, museum openings, and symphony performances. That she would one day be involved in running a sports and recreation promotion never entered her head.

"Then I shall take that as a compliment," she told the man standing before her. "It seems I've succeeded."

She started to walk away, but his next words made her stop and turn.

"Oh, you haven't completely succeeded yet," he said.

"I beg your pardon," she answered. "You may know something about flying planes, and. . .and jumping out of them, but what makes you say I haven't succeeded? In just a few hours all the exhibits will be in place."

"And the airplane, Miss Marsh?" He smiled mysteriously.

"Especially the airplane, Mr. Barry." In another moment she feared she might finally lose her temper with this man, so she turned deliberately on her heel and walked away. At any rate, it was time to find Red Johnson and Ed Kozinsky and see what was holding up the airplane from taxiing onto the mall.

As she walked, Kelly regretted her harsh thoughts about Steven Barry. She tried hard to remember her upbringing and live up to the beliefs of her church, to be charitable, kind, and forgiving, but sometimes she failed. And almost always, she decided, a man was the cause of her failure.

She returned to the parking lot where Kozinsky, Johnson, and two other men dressed in work clothes were deep in conversation.

Kozinsky said, "I'm sure it will fit."

"With a crowbar?" Johnson asked. "The fuselage will go through the opening, but not the wings." He stalked to the back of the plane, squatted down, and peered at the opening between the buildings beyond, as if visualizing how the plane would fit between them.

"Maybe if you went sideways," Kozinsky suggested. He picked up the tail gear and began to walk slowly to his left, the plane rotating in a half circle as he did so. Then he stooped down and looked at the opening the plane would have to clear.

"It's too long," Johnson said. "Anyway, you can't drive it in sideways! I tell you it can't be done."

Kelly felt queasy. After all this trouble, would she really be frustrated at the last minute and not be able to have the plane in the exhibit? Steven Barry had just hinted she wouldn't have the plane on the mall; could he be right after all? Had he known the plane wouldn't fit?

She stopped herself. Negative thinking would not show her the solution to this problem.

"There must be a way," she said, approaching the men,

speaking softly, calmly, trying to be confident. "You did promise me, you know."

"I know," Johnson answered, "and I will do it, even if I have to take the wings off to get her in."

"Take off the wings?" This seemingly impossible suggestion made Kelly's voice rise. Still, perhaps that was the answer.

"Yes, we can take them off out here, push her onto the mall, and then put the wings back on."

"How long will that take?" Already a pale blue sky announced the approach of morning.

"Couple of hours," Johnson said.

"Altogether?"

"No, a couple of hours to take them off and a couple more to put them back on again."

"But we don't have that much time," Kelly protested. "It's almost six now. Everything must be ready by 9:30!"

"Maybe we can do it in a little less time."

"That's not all; this parking lot will start to fill up by nine. I can't have this going on then." She held her voice under control with difficulty, knowing the problems she faced.

"We can rope off this area of the lot," Kozinsky suggested.

"That's not the worst of it," Kelly continued. "I need the plane in position first, because of the other exhibits that go after it. If the boats and trailered vehicles are on the mall first, you'll never be able to maneuver the plane into place."

"I'm sorry," Johnson said, shaking his head. "I guess I should have started out even earlier this morning. I suppose I should have anticipated that we might have to do this."

Kelly fought down the temptation to blame Kozinsky;

she had told him her plan and he should have known its feasibility. But blame wouldn't get the plane on the mall any faster. Besides, in the back of her mind, she had to admit this was her fault as well; she should have told Kozinsky to measure the opening precisely so she could have given the measurements to Red Johnson. Then they would have known in plenty of time. Her problems all came from not being familiar with this type of thing; she just couldn't anticipate all the difficulties that might occur.

Once again she brought her thoughts back into line. She must show thanks and gratitude to both Kozinsky and Johnson, who were doing their best to solve this particular problem.

"Don't blame yourselves," she said, "but please start right away and do it as quickly as you can. When you have the plane inside, take it straight to its location before you put the wings back on; that may save some time." She smiled encouragingly at them. Now she must hope that her boss wouldn't come to the center to observe. Somehow she would have to keep the other vehicles waiting while this operation took place, even if it did seem hopelessly complicated.

Suddenly she heard the deep voice of Steven Barry. "Hold it," he said to Johnson as he and his companion began to work on the plane. "You don't have to do that."

"I can't get the plane in any other way," Johnson explained. "This is the widest area onto the mall, and it still won't fit."

"That's right," Kelly added. Having accepted Red Johnson's solution, she wanted to get on with it. "This is the widest opening. If it won't go through here, there's no way to get the plane on the mall, except by taking off the wings."

"I wouldn't be so hasty, if I were you," he drawled, staring pointedly at Kelly. "I don't think you've explored all the options."

"I really think we have."

Steven ignored her comment and continued to smile. "I've just been around the mall and there's a much better way."

Kelly was thoroughly upset by this time. In addition to the other frustrations, why did she also have to be plagued with this skydiver, who seemed convinced he knew all about everything? "I'm afraid there is no other way," she said.

"Begging your pardon," he said, with mock courtesy, "between those two buildings on the south side, where the planter is, would be a much better choice."

"Mr. Kozinsky and I checked that out already," Kelly answered. "The distance between the building and the sculpture that stands in that planter is much narrower than this opening. If it won't fit through here, it certainly won't fit there."

"It will if you raise the plane. There's a ramp in place on that side already, next to the curb. All you have to do is put the ramps against the planter ledge, push the tail gear of the plane onto that, and keep the front gear off the ground. Four of us can manage that. Then the wings will clear the sculpture."

Kelly had been waiting for him to finish speaking, so that she could present counter arguments, but suddenly she found herself visualizing his proposal. It might work. She hated to admit this particular man might be right; he had annoyed her from his very first sentence. Still, she could not allow pride to stall things. She had to get that plane on the mall, even if it meant choosing Steven Barry's plan.

Silently, everyone waited for her decision.

"Let's try that," she said. "It hadn't occurred to me to consider raising the airplane's wings. . ."

"Perfectly understandable," Steven Barry said, circling her fingers with his. "You're merely a girl. Girls can't be expected to know about things like this." And he squeezed her hand, then dropped it and walked away, leaving her perplexed and angry.

Why had he said such a thing to her? Red Johnson hadn't seen the possibility of doing that either, until Steven Barry pointed it out. Why single her out and criticize her for not thinking of it? What a conceited, arrogant. . .

Her face burned, and she bit her lip to keep from saying the harsh words that sprang to her mind and tongue. She closed her eyes tightly and remembered that a Christian should be charitable. If only they had got the plane on the mall as originally planned. If only Johnson had driven it over instead of this exasperating skydiver. If only she'd never laid eyes on him!

Well, she consoled herself, she'd never have to see him again.

But the hand he had just held still tingled from his touch.

two

Lyle Durning perched on the edge of Kelly's dark walnut desk and beamed at her.

"You see," he said, a smile creasing his round face, "I told you you could do it; it was a great promotion!"

"Thanks," Kelly said. She had never worked so hard preparing anything: all the reading, investigating, phone calling, traveling to so many places, arranging so many details. Just thinking about it now almost made her tired all over again. She had put in three incredible weeks of effort for an event that lasted only four days. And now, on Monday morning, she sat in her office again, and her boss was pleased with the results.

Yet she knew in her heart she could not bask in his compliments. Steven Barry was the one who had solved her biggest problem—getting the airplane on the mall. An unpleasant sensation nagged her, for she had to admit to herself that he had not only solved her problem, but she had been tremendously attracted to his good looks as well. His attitude, however, had been totally obnoxious, and she thought of him almost with loathing.

Lyle left her desk and paced the floor, hands thrust deep inside his trouser pockets.

"I knew you were right for that job. And I have an even better one. Imagine twelve weeks of promotions all on one central theme. You'll do all the arrangements, news releases, posters, advertising, for something that's never been done in this part of the state."

"The opera promotion?" Kelly's heart leapt.

But Lyle wasn't listening. He walked around, gesturing and talking quickly. "I like to play hunches, and most of the time they're good ones. The shopping center sports promotion, for example, paid off. It proved that you needed to be taken out of your rut and have your abilities challenged."

"Just what is it you want me to do?" Kelly asked, worried that perhaps it wasn't the opera promotion after all. But what else could it be? She had put her name down for it weeks ago; she had listed her qualifications. Still, her knees felt weak and butterflies threatened to start up in her stomach.

"Skydiving," Lyle said.

"Skydiving? Lyle, you can't mean it!" Another sports theme, and a completely ridiculous sport at that.

Lyle continued, unaware of Kelly's turmoil, "Actually, it's thanks to you that this worked out. I met the skydiver at your promotion last weekend and signed him to a three-month contract. He's going to give exhibitions for six promotions in twelve weeks, and you're going to travel with him and promote the whole thing. He's the best skydiver in the state, maybe the whole country. His name is Steven Barry."

Visions of Steven Barry floated before her eyes: that maddening, arrogant giant of a man, with eyes the color of blue marbles, a mocking smile on his lips. The butterflies in her stomach turned into bees—painful, stinging bees—that were attacking her from inside.

"I can't possibly do that." Kelly rose from her chair, hands shaking. "I only did the sports promotion for you because I wanted to cooperate. I wasn't qualified then and I'm not now." Her body trembled with the intensity of her plea, and she thought the beating of her heart must be visible beneath the pale pink summer dress she wore.

Lyle Durning's tone was kind, but firm. "Come now, Kelly; you're not going to tell me you're incompetent when you managed to put on one of the best sports promotions I've ever seen?"

With a great effort, Kelly composed herself. She thrust to the back of her mind the thought that she never wanted to see Steven Barry again. "I'm certainly glad it turned out well," she said, softening her voice. "But if it did, it was pure luck. I really knew nothing about sports; I still don't."

"But perhaps that's where you had an advantage," Lyle said, coming forward and putting his hands on her shoulders, as if direct physical contact would impress her more favorably with his viewpoint. "Other promotion directors might have been inhibited by what has been done in the past. They might have chosen the old ways—the uninspired ways—of going about it. But you—knowing nothing, as you admitted—started with a fresh eye. You didn't know certain things had never been done, so you went ahead and did them. You broke new ground."

"But a lucky accident," she protested, "is no reason to give me similar assignments in the future."

"I don't think it was an accident," Lyle said. "I think you have a natural flair for this kind of thing. That's why I don't want you to say no to this skydiving tour. I'm convinced you can bring some new and exciting twists to it."

Kelly moved away from her boss, so that his arms fell from her shoulders. She barely knew the man, and although she felt his gesture to be one of mere friendship, it made her uncomfortable. Almost as uncomfortable as the thought of working daily with Steven Barry!

"I think you're wrong," she answered, turning toward

the window and looking out at the other office buildings across the street. "I don't think I have a flair for it at all. And if I can put some imagination to work, then why not let me do it on a promotion I really enjoy and know something about? Why not let me do that with the opera project?"

"I've been meaning to talk to you about that," Lyle said, running his short fingers through his sandy hair and seating himself in the chair before Kelly's desk. "The opera promotion has been postponed, perhaps indefinitely. It's a very expensive proposition and, so far, we haven't been able to find enough sponsors to come up with the necessary money."

Kelly's spirits fell even further. She had had such hopes for the opera promotion.

"We're still contacting organizations which might help," Lyle went on, "but I have no idea when any conclusion will be reached. In the meantime, I need you to take this new project."

"But you said it will be twelve weeks long. If the opera promotion begins before then, I'll be tied up and won't be able to do it. And I've looked forward to this for almost a year."

"I don't see how we can revive the opera thing in six months, much less twelve weeks," Lyle said, "but I promise you that if something breaks before then, I'll let you know."

Kelly saw a glimmer of hope. Perhaps the promotion she had looked forward to would merely be postponed and would take place later. If she acceded to this request, Lyle would surely give her the assignment in the future. "All right," she said, coming back to her desk. "Do I understand this is a promise? If I do the skydiving promotion, you'll let me handle the opera benefit, no matter when that comes up?"

Lyle laughed. "Yes, I promise. Do you want it in writing?"

"No, a simple handshake will do."

She smiled and held out her hand, and Lyle rose from the chair and took it into his. He held it a trifle longer than necessary, and looking into her eyes, he said, "Why don't we seal our bargain over dinner tonight?"

Kelly removed her hand quickly. "Oh, I don't think so." She groped for an excuse for why she couldn't have dinner with him. He was nice looking, young, single, and he had just promised to give her what she wanted. Still, something held her back.

"When I worked in Minnesota," he said, "my group always did that on Friday evenings. We'd have a simple dinner together at the end of the week, discuss what we had accomplished, what loomed in the future. It made us feel like a team."

"It sounds fine," Kelly said, stalling. "Maybe some other time. Right now I have plans for tonight. And anyway," she added, laughing self-consciously, "it isn't even Friday."

"Well, how about Friday?" he persisted.

"I may go home this weekend," she said. "My mother lives in southern California and I sort of promised her..." It wasn't exactly a lie, she told herself, because her mother had asked her to come down that weekend, and she had stalled, not giving an unequivocal yes or no.

"Well," Lyle said, starting to leave, "I'll have my secretary bring you the information we have on the skydiving promotion and you can start on it right away. I expect you'll want to go out to the airport this afternoon and meet Mr. Barry. I told him we'd start today."

"You told him? This afternoon?" Kelly retained her composure with difficulty.

"Six promotions in twelve weeks, remember?" Lyle opened her door and stood with one hand on the knob. Pointing a finger at her, he added, "The sooner you get it done, the sooner you can do the opera thing, right?" He closed the door behind him.

Kelly slumped back into her chair. Lyle had evidently been sure he could persuade her to take the job, but why had he signed Steven Barry, of all the skydivers in the world? How ironic that her own promotion—her insistence on having an airplane on the mall—had enabled Lyle to meet Steven and set this up.

Still, she really had no choice. As the boss, Lyle could order her to do anything, under threat of firing her. Only courtesy suggested that the division manager ask what promotions you wanted to handle; in actual fact you could be assigned to anything, though her former boss had never insisted she do anything she didn't like. She guessed she was being tested. The job had all been too easy before, doing what interested her. Now she'd have to grow and learn. She ought to be grateful for the opportunity—and she would be, except for Steven Barry.

She thought about Lyle's suggestion that they have dinner together. Maybe he did that with people in his last job, but that didn't mean he could carry the practice over to this one. Still, to give him the benefit of the doubt, she couldn't really call his motive far-fetched. Many people did meet socially with their co-workers. Perhaps the idea had some value. It didn't necessarily mean he was flirting with her. And besides, when it came down to which man she would rather see—Lyle Durning or Steven Barry— Lyle would win any day.

But fretting about Mr. Barry would get her nowhere. She would have to learn to like the man—or at least get along with him—for twelve weeks.

Her thoughts were interrupted by Lyle's secretary coming in and dropping an enormous pile of material on her desk, and for the next three hours she read, studied, and made notes.

Early in the afternoon she got into her car and pointed it in the direction of the airport. Trees in their bright green leaves arched overhead, and the scent of flowers filled the air. As she drove, she thought of how she liked this little town and how glad she was that her church project of making cassette tapes for the blind had led her into public relations work and finally brought her here. The people were friendly, and the church she had joined became a second home where she could continue the volunteer work.

Almost before she knew it, Kelly arrived at the airport and saw to her left a red and white sign that read, "Flyway Aviation." She parked her car near the small redwood building and entered the double doors. The small office had a broad counter blocking half the space, but no occupants.

She waited a few minutes, then rapped her knuckles lightly on the counter, and waited again, but still no one appeared. Noticing another door at the rear of the small office, she walked around the counter and opened it. It led to the airfield, and she strolled toward the hangars. Before her on the tarmac sat several planes of various types and sizes, and a few men were visible, some working on planes, some just standing about talking. None, however, was Steven Barry.

Farther out on the field she saw a man in a jumpsuit and three young girls in tee-shirts and jeans striding onto the grassy field; from his bright hair shining in the sun, Kelly recognized Red Johnson. He walked to a large circle marked out on the ground. She saw him retreat a few paces and stop and look up at the sky. The girls surrounding him also looked up. Curious, Kelly did the same.

A small plane, rather like the one that had come to the shopping center mall, flew above, and then something fell from an open door on its side. Involuntarily, she gasped.

The falling object became wider and she realized, heart pounding, that it was a man. Or, at any rate, a person. He or she had jumped from the plane and now fell through the air, arms and legs outstretched. Something attached to his back leaped upward, and Kelly saw a tiny white piece of cloth that resembled a miniature parachute. Even before she could wonder how he'd be saved from certain death by that small scrap of cloth, the tiny chute pulled more fabric out of the backpack, and then a beautiful orange and white canopy blossomed above the figure. As it billowed out in the sky, the person was jerked from his prone position into an upright one and slowly glided toward earth.

Eyes riveted to the scene above her, Kelly realized with surprise that there were holes in the parachute, huge empty spaces between the gores of the canopy.

She ran to Red Johnson's side. "Why are there holes in the parachute?"

Johnson turned his head and acknowledged her. "That's how he guides it," he answered. "Air comes in through those openings and when he pulls on the lines, it makes the parachute change direction. Actually, that's an old type; the newer ones are different, and much better. Watch now, in a moment he'll land right here. He's the best; he never misses a target."

Sure enough, the skydiver descended lower and lower and then landed right in the center of the circle, his knees flexing as he touched the ground. Immediately on landing, he pulled the collapsing parachute to the ground.

The young girls ran over to him, but Kelly stood still, though she felt surprisingly excited by what she had just witnessed. She had seen brief shots of skydiving in films, but it had never moved her. In fact she only thought it stupid—deliberately jumping out of a perfectly good airplane—but there was something awe-inspiring about seeing it in person. She realized she was perspiring, and her breath came in gasps. She wanted to rush over to thank the man or congratulate him, she didn't know quite which. Instead she continued to stare, and then, as he finished rolling the parachute into a manageable bundle, the girls departed, and he came walking toward her. She saw, with a mixture of fear, embarrassment, and a strange sort of delight, that he was Steven Barry.

She swallowed a lump in her throat, stared at him with open mouth, and then he stood in front of her, smiling down. Her heart skipped a beat.

"Hello," she said nervously. "That was. . .wonderful."

"Thank you." His expression turned to one of skepticism, and he handed his rolled-up chute to Red Johnson, who walked off the field with it, leaving them alone.

"You surprise me," he said. "I certainly didn't expect you to turn up here. You seemed rather less than pleased with me at Park Side Shopping Center—but now I find you watching me make a jump like any teen aged 'groupie.'"

Kelly's pleasure in his jump and his expertise in landing on target faded in a moment. Did he imagine she had any interest in him personally? She had been right in her first estimation of the man; he was definitely conceited.

"I congratulate you for a beautiful exhibition," she said, her tone cool, "but I didn't come here today to become part of your admiring audience. My presence is strictly business."

"Oh?" he said, questioning. "Did Ingersoll Productions decide to do a sports promotion here at the airport? I must admit it would make more sense than at a shopping center."

"I'm afraid you know little about public relations work," she answered, her lips turning into a tiny smile, "but that's perfectly understandable. Skydivers can't be expected to know about things like this."

He paused, and Kelly knew, by the look in his eyes and by his own smile, that he recognized his very words from their last meeting. "Then perhaps you can teach me," he said, his face softening. "I like learning new things."

"It will be my pleasure. But not just now. I'm here to discuss the skydiving tour you're doing for Ingersoll."

"Why didn't Mr. Durning come himself? Are you his secretary?"

Her annoyance returned, just when she had begun to feel they might call a truce to their bickering after all. "As I told you the other day, I'm nobody's secretary. I'm a P.R. director, and furthermore, I'm in charge of this tour."

"In charge of *this* tour?" he thundered, his belligerent attitude toward her returning in full force. "You, who couldn't get that airplane on the mall?"

"I would have got it on the mall," Kelly said, her face coloring, she was sure, to the shade of her dress. "Anyway," she continued, forcing herself to calm down again, "the rest of the promotion concluded very successfully."

"Maybe so," he admitted, "but that doesn't mean you're qualified to handle my tour."

"I wish you'd stop accusing me of being no more than a slow-witted child. I'm perfectly qualified. Like you, I enjoy learning new things, and whatever is necessary for this project, rest assured, I will learn."

"Well, I don't have time to teach you."

"I don't expect you to."

"That figures," he said, disgustedly. "I suppose you're going to read *books* on the subject!"

Kelly's temper finally exploded. No matter how hard she tried to be polite to this man, he seemed determined to upset her.

"One doesn't have to commit murder in order to write a mystery novel," she answered, "although perhaps, since you don't read, that analogy escapes you. Let me find one closer to your limited experience. You don't have to lay an egg to know good ones from bad!"

His smile again flickered across his face, and she thought he would laugh. Instead, he simply waited, studying her, for what seemed long minutes.

Immediately she regretted her outburst. She had been taught to turn the other cheek. "I'm sorry," she began.

Without replying, he took her hand in his and led her to the runway.

"What are you doing? Where are we going?" she asked, almost running to keep up with his long strides.

"I'm going to give you a test," he shouted over his shoulder. "If you pass it, you can come along on the tour."

"A test?" she gasped, and she tried to stop, but his momentum didn't allow it, and instead she merely stumbled in her high heels. His hand went around her waist, holding her up; then he continued his purposeful journey. Even while trying to keep from tripping again, she realized he was leading her to the airplane which had just landed. No doubt it was the same one from which he had made his jump.

Suddenly the meaning of his words came to her, and she felt drained of life. Did he mean to take her up and force her to parachute from the plane before admitting she could do her job?

Her heart pounded. "No, you wouldn't!" she gasped.

"Wouldn't I?" he jeered.

"I've never done it before. I couldn't possibly!"

"Not flown?" he asked. "I don't believe you," and he continued his fast pace.

"Jumped from a plane!" she shouted at his back.

He stopped dead, the suddenness almost knocking her down, and turned glaring eyes on her. "Jump? Do you actually think I'd let you jump? That's the craziest thing I ever heard."

"But, I thought. . .I mean. . ." Kelly felt thoroughly confused, even as relief flooded over her.

He seemed to study her face and then relaxed and smiled. "Either you know even less about skydiving than I gave you credit for—which proves my point in objecting to your handling this promotion—or else you have an excessively low opinion of me."

She merely stared at the ground, feeling stupid, confused, and terrified all at once.

"You do think I'm a beast, don't you?" he asked. Still, she remained silent. "Well, I can't blame you; I've been somewhat less than polite to you. But I wouldn't let my worst enemy make a jump without training, certainly not a beautiful woman like you."

Again Kelly was surprised. One moment the man was insulting and almost brutal, the next apologetic and complimentary, a definite enigma.

"Then what did you mean?" she asked.

"I merely planned to take you for an airplane ride. I admit

I had thought of doing a few aerobatics and perhaps frightening you out of your wits, but now I think I'd better made it a gentle, easy flight."

"Don't change your plans on my account," she said. "I admit the prospect of parachuting frightened me, but I've flown in planes before, and I can take anything you can dish out!"

Instantly she regretted her bravado. She had never flown in anything but a commercial airliner—and on only two occasions at that; he could certainly scare her if he did stunts in this small plane.

"We'll see," he said as they reached the red and white Cessna. "I'm taking her up," he said to the pilot just exiting from the craft, and then he helped Kelly climb into the plane.

She was acutely aware of having to take a rather large step up, made awkward by her high heels and dress. She wanted to clutch her skirt to her thighs but instead had to hold onto a support.

"Yes, indeed," Steven drawled, his expression confirming her worst suspicions, "I think I'll make it a safe and sane flight. I'd hate to do anything to risk damaging legs like those!"

Kelly blushed furiously, but thankfully the skydiver couldn't see her face as he closed the door and went around to the other side, then climbed in beside her.

He fastened his own seat belt and then made sure she had fastened hers. Kelly found herself once again aware of the attraction his physical presence had for her. When he brushed her arm to reach for the seat belt buckle, she reacted as if a searing fire had touched her; the closeness of his body in the tiny plane made her almost giddy.

Get hold of yourself, Kelly, she scolded; she made an

effort to keep her mind on the cockpit and its many instruments instead of him. She was unsuccessful, though; she simply couldn't concentrate. He turned switches and dials, the engine leapt into life, making a horrendous noise that almost drowned out her thoughts, and the small plane taxied forward.

After a few moments, Steven pushed the throttle all the way forward, and the plane tore down the runway. Suddenly it ascended, and the sense of motion disappeared. Only by looking out the window on her side could she detect the movement of the plane, watching the land drop away beneath them. Looking to the front, seeing only blue sky and puffy white clouds in the distance, she had no sensation of travel at all. It was as if she were sitting in a giant rocking chair in the sky.

The noise prevented any conversation, but she looked at Steven, found him looking at her too, and turned quickly away, staring out the side window again. As they flew over the nearby farms and fields, rectangular patches of color— greens, browns, golds—replaced the runway that had been below a moment ago. What a difference from flying in a commercial plane—no wonder pilots loved to fly—what a feeling of freedom, of power!

The flight lasted at least fifteen minutes, but to Kelly it seemed only seconds. Suddenly they swooshed down toward the runway again, then the plane seemed to stall, and she felt a bump as the wheels touched the ground. After they taxied for some seconds, Steven turned off the engine. In the silence that followed, he said, "Well, smooth enough for you?"

"Too smooth," she said, still unwilling to admit her relief. "I told you you didn't have to baby me, Mr. Barry."

"Perhaps I want to. And the name is Steven, remember?"

His voice was soft, but the look in his eyes intimidated her. He appeared to be smirking, to be aware of her thoughts and of how attractive he was to women.

She unfastened her seat belt and reached for the door handle. "Thanks for the ride, but I really think we should get down to business."

Steven slipped from his own seat and climbed from the cockpit, then came around to help her down. His hand took hers firmly, but his eyes held a look she couldn't fathom.

Instead of merely helping her alight, he put both hands on her waist and lifted her from the plane, setting her feet on the tarmac in front of him. Then he bent his head to hers and kissed her firmly.

His warm lips were surprisingly smooth. His hard muscled body, so close to hers, sent shivers through her, and Kelly found her mouth clinging to his, even though her hands pressed against his broad chest. He released her at last and their eyes met. Then he said, smiling, "I think we're going to work very well together after all, Kelly."

Her defenses were in place at once. "Not that way! Don't ever do that again!" She stalked off the field, head high, cheeks burning.

three

Kelly half walked, half ran back to the office of Flyway Aviation, not knowing if Steven followed her and what her next move should be. She breathed rapidly and felt her heart beating faster. His kiss had caused a reaction that surprised her with its intensity; she must compose herself.

The picture of an angel painted on a door caught her eye. Assuming it was the ladies' room, she went inside. Staring at her flushed face in the mirror, she reproached herself for reacting as she had. But he was certainly the strangest man she had ever met. What made him behave the way he did?

Running fingers through her tousled hair, she admitted she looked attractive enough—but Steven seemed more eager to offend than to please. He had probably decided to alienate her, either with unpleasant behavior or unwanted attentions, so that she would resign from handling his sky-diving promotion. He had made no secret of the fact that he didn't think her competent. If he actually felt attracted to her, then he had certainly chosen a poor way of showing it. Where was the gentleness, the tender devotion, of someone who was falling in love? No, obviously he was only trying to make her angry.

She closed her eyes tightly, trying to decide how to handle the situation. She couldn't see herself telling Lyle she was quitting the promotion. Not at least until she had tried to straighten the situation out herself. Her resolve firm, she opened her eyes, took a deep breath, and left the room.

Steven Barry sat at a desk behind the counter, but he got to his feet when he saw her emerge from the ladies' room. "Kelly, please let me apologize."

She paused before speaking. The apology was welcome, but she remained suspicious of the man's motives. "Did Mr. Johnson put you up to this?"

He neither affirmed nor denied her accusation. "You make it very difficult for me to acquire the proper repentant attitude."

"Are you through playing games with me?"

"What do you mean?"

"Will you stop harassing me? Will you finally acknowledge that I know my job and let me do it without any more problems?"

"I wouldn't call kissing you a problem. I would call it pleasant. But yes, I'm resigned to your handling the tour."

"Then we're agreed," Kelly said, relaxing.

"Are we?" He flashed a broad, mischievous smile. "In that case, I'll assume you enjoyed my kiss."

"I didn't mean that!" she said quickly. "I meant—"

"I know what you meant," he interrupted. "But I've already explained that I like to do things I shouldn't. I'm willing to accept you as the public relations person on my tours, but I can't absolutely guarantee that I won't forget occasionally and try to kiss you again."

"Do you consider it some sort of challenge?" Kelly asked.

"Perhaps. I've never believed in taking life too seriously. You ought to live each moment to the fullest, and I don't like to think of missing out on too many pleasant experiences."

"I should think you never do miss any."

Steven laughed again. "Tell me how you became such a serious person so young. Were you raised in poverty and had to fight your way to the top?"

"No," Kelly said, "I just want people to accept me for what I am: a competent, reasonably intelligent person, not a. . ." She groped for the right word. She didn't want to say anything that might be taken wrong.

He finished the sentence for her. "A beautiful woman? But why not? You are, you know, so why try to hide it?"

"In the first place, I'm not beautiful. And in the second, character and integrity are far more important. Personality—"

"I like your personality too," he said, grinning impishly.

Kelly ignored his interruption. "As for my background, I come from an ordinary middle-class family, a devout Christian family," she added.

Steven's eyebrows arched. "One of those."

"I'm proud of it, regardless of what you may think."

His expression underwent a change, but he didn't speak.

Kelly continued, anxious to explain herself. "I've always been active in my church, and besides working my job, I volunteer my time to read to the blind and make cassette tapes for them."

"Admirable, I'm sure," he said, "but I'm afraid you're getting too serious again. Somehow I don't want to talk about character and integrity when I'm with you." His glance took in her entire form and he grinned; then, in spite of his earlier words, he became serious. "However, you're kinder to me than I deserve, and I apologize for everything I said or did that annoyed you. I won't bore you with the details of how I became such an insensitive blockhead— but I certainly shouldn't have taken my frustrations out on you. I'm sorry." He paused, waiting for her answer.

Realizing his apology probably had not come easily, Kelly felt he had finally offered the truce she had been hoping for. "You're forgiven," she said. She wanted to add, "But . . ." and rehearse all those maddening aspects of his character he had revealed so far, but she held her peace.

"Good. I'm ready to work with you, and I promise not to make any more chauvinistic comments. I know they were stupid and unfounded. I'm sure you're very good at your job."

Kelly sat down in the worn leather swivel chair he indicated. "Promotional work is not gender-based, even in the area of what are normally considered male-dominated sports," she said in the tone of someone making a speech.

"I understand. There are even quite a few women skydivers; I've trained seven myself."

"I'm glad to hear it."

He turned his steely blue eyes on her, and a question seemed to lurk behind them. After a pause, he went on. "Actually, aside from your not looking the part, I thought I detected a note of defensiveness in your attitude last week—that you weren't exactly overjoyed with the assignment."

Kelly looked down a moment, nervously fingering the folds in her skirt, as she formed an answer. She endeavored always to be honest, yet she didn't want Steven to think she wouldn't be enthusiastic about their tour and do her absolute best.

"My background hasn't been in those areas, of course— but promoting a sports event is remarkably similar to promoting, say, an opera benefit."

As soon as she mentioned it, she wished she hadn't said the word "opera." Her hands mechanically creased and uncreased the fabric of her skirt, but by the time she recognized her nervous gesture and stopped, Steven had made the connection.

"You'd rather be doing an opera benefit than this?"

When she didn't answer immediately, he added, "Is there such a promotion and did you get switched to mine against your will?"

Kelly looked up at him. "It's not like that at all. The opera benefit might never occur; there are funding problems. But if it is, I've been promised I can supervise it. Now, let's get down to our own business—"

But Steven refused to budge from the previous topic. He leaned forward, muscled arms resting on his knees. "What kind of funding problems?"

"The usual kind, start-up money, unless a backer will help in the beginning. Later, of course, we expect it to pay for itself. But I really don't have time to discuss that. I'm sure you're not interested."

"Oh, but I am. Perhaps I can help."

"I don't understand. How could you help?" Kelly pictured Steven—indeed everyone who worked at the airport—as barely making a living, but sticking it out for love of flying.

"I have a few connections," he went on, straightening in his chair and tipping it back, catching the underside of hers with one black-booted foot, imprisoning her between chair and desk. "Have you ever head of Christopher Trask?"

Kelly thought a moment. "The name sounds familiar."

"He's the richest man in the valley."

Her eyebrows arched.

"And he's a member of the Society for the Arts."

A smile began at the corners of her lips. Of course, *that* Christopher Trask. "You know him?" she asked, surprised.

"I once worked for him."

"As. . . ?" she prompted.

"General flunky." He grunted. "But I think I know him

pretty well, nevertheless. Your opera thing would appeal to him, I'm sure. You ought to try."

"I will. I'll write to him as soon as—"

"No," Steven interrupted, "go to see him in person. Believe me, that will have the best results. Do it right away, today."

Kelly stood, and Steven was forced to move his legs or create the impression she was his captive.

"You seem very anxious," she said, walking to the wide office window, frowning slightly. "It almost sounds as if you're trying to get rid of me."

Steven rose quickly, his chair banging on the floor. "Now let's not start that again. I said I'm sorry for my earlier behavior and I meant it. I really *want* to work with you."

Kelly turned and silently studied his rugged features.

"You're very suspicious," he continued. "I'm just trying to do a favor, make up a little for the way I treated you before."

Her face warm, Kelly looked away again. How incredible that this man, of all people, should remind her to be a gracious recipient. "You're right, and I do accept it. Thank you."

"Fine. You will go to see him then? Today?"

"Yes, I'll see him," she said, "but only if we finish here first. If you keep changing the subject, we'll *never* get done."

Steven laughed. "Agreed. What do I do now, teacher?"

Kelly pulled her pocket calendar from her purse and sat down again; for the next hour, she and Steven pencilled in dates and places for his exhibition jumps and discussed the logistics of other skydivers, airplanes, and airport clearances.

&

Christopher Trask did not live in town, but in the country. The drive took Kelly through the rolling hills that were already beginning to turn gold, their summer color, although dotted with deep green trees. Along the highway, the pink and white oleanders in the dividers added more color, contrasting with the occasional deep purple of a flowering plum tree.

Only vaguely aware of the beauty of the summer afternoon, she rehearsed what she'd say to Mr. Trask, how she would urge him to sponsor the opera program, what it would mean to the area.

She thought of Steven. How ironic that his suggestion might be the means of releasing her from the responsibility for his own tour. Whether he proposed it for that reason or not, the results would be the same. She would have what she wanted, and also be rid of Steven and his skydiving. His pleasant attitude during the past hour had not completely dispelled her discomfort around the man, and she felt things would be simpler if their paths did not cross again.

Almost an hour later, she slowed the speed of her compact car and turned off the main highway onto a side road, then Trask Drive. That, Kelly thought, is the ultimate test of wealth: that people name streets after you.

But Trask Drive was not heavily populated. The houses were so widely spaced that she could literally not see two of them at once. When she reached a fork in the road, a sign on the left stated, "Trask Circle—Not a Through Street." Turning between the stone gates, Kelly proceeded up the steep hill, suddenly besieged with doubts. What if he wasn't home today? She should have telephoned ahead to make an appointment, and she mentally berated herself for not thinking of it. He might be too busy to see her. A thousand reasons why her trip would be wasted came flooding into her mind. How impetuous she had been to simply jump in her car and drive so far to see him. Usually she was much more organized and practical.

She could not back down now, but her palms were moist on the wheel of the car, and she felt silky strands of hair cling to the nape of her neck.

The house came into view, a three-storied mansion, ivy clinging to its gray stone sides. It stood at the top of a rise, its lawn like green carpet. A garage for five cars, with a second floor above it, flanked a greenhouse, its many panes gleaming in the sun.

The driveway wound through trees, and Kelly occasionally lost sight of the house. Her attention was suddenly riveted back to the road when a small red sports car appeared directly in her path. She reacted instantly, swerving the steering wheel sharply to the right and going off the road onto the grassy bank. Her breathing almost stopped, her throat tightened.

As the sports car zoomed past, she glimpsed the other driver. It was a girl; even in that split second, Kelly saw a pale face framed by jet-black hair. The car sped away, and Kelly maneuvered back onto the drive again, with little time to wonder about the identity of this person and why she drove so fast on the wrong side of the road.

The gravel driveway crunched under her tires, and she stopped in front of the mansion. She got out of the car, went up the two steps, and rang the doorbell. A butler opened the solid black door.

"I'm Kelly Marsh," she said, handing him a business card. "I'd like to see Mr. Trask."

He ushered her through a large hallway with a polished black and white terrazzo floor; then, after she had waited a few moments while he disappeared into another room, he led her into the most beautiful room she had ever seen. Ceiling-to-floor mullioned windows flooded the room with light, revealing panelled walls, antique furniture covered in exquisite silk fabrics, and a huge marble-topped fireplace with a painted landscape above it. In a chair by the fire, although no blaze glowed from its depths, sat an elderly white-haired man, wearing a deep red smoking jacket with black satin lapels, a blue knitted robe over his legs.

"Excuse me for not rising," Trask said, as Kelly entered the room. "I regret that my health doesn't always allow me the privilege of being courteous to beautiful ladies any longer."

The speech impressed Kelly as much as the man, whose smiling face was smooth, almost unlined, and aristocratic.

"You're very kind to let me come," Kelly said, going to him and offering her hand. "And I'm sorry you're not feeling well."

He took hers in one of his surprisingly strong and firm hands, using the other to wave aside her concern. He pointed to a nearby chair and urged her to be seated. "Having visitors always makes me feel better."

Kelly introduced herself, reflecting that Mr. Trask seemed very gracious. His great wealth, evidenced by the magnificent home, had not made him cold and aloof; he appeared genuinely glad of her presence. Even this huge room seemed somehow cozy.

"I've come to ask for your help," she said.

"I am at your service," Trask replied. "If there is anything an old man can do, that is." He chuckled dryly.

"I understand," she began, "that you are a member of the Society for the Arts."

"I founded that organization almost fifty years ago," he

said, "and I'm happy to say it has done some good in its time."

"A great deal of good. The list of its activities would fill a book. That's why I thought you might be willing to consider aid to an opera promotion."

"Opera?" the man repeated.

"Yes, we've never had an opera in the valley. One has to go all the way to Los Angeles or San Francisco to see one."

"You're right. My late wife loved the opera, but of course I haven't attended for a long time."

"We've had musical comedies but not by professionals. The high schools do them, and East Valley College puts on a very nice show every year—but nothing of the caliber of the production I'm talking about. For this we need a real opera company, and I have one that has agreed to come. We even have an auditorium in town that can be converted into an opera house with very little effort. All we need is a sponsor to underwrite the cost and guarantee the salaries for the company. But I'm sure it would pay for itself once it got started."

Kelly paused after this long speech and wondered, in the silence that followed, if her breathing was as loud to Mr. Trask as it sounded to her.

"Tell me more about it," he replied, "over tea." He reached to the small, round table at his side and rang a silver bell.

"Thank you very much." Kelly hadn't expected this, but his request thrilled her. It was definitely an encouraging sign.

The next hour flew by. The butler brought in a tray laden with tiny sandwiches, petit fours, nut bread with sweet butter, and fresh fruit. Her charming host seemed interested in everything Kelly had to say, asking questions about her project, as well as about her own background. He put her so at ease that she almost felt as if she were with her father again.

Finally, aware she had been talking while Mr. Trask did the listening, she apologized. "I'm sorry; I seem to be monopolizing the conversation."

"Not at all, my dear," he said, reaching across the table and patting her hand. "I don't see many visitors these days." A frown appeared on his forehead, only to be chased away at once. "At least not any as interesting as you."

Kelly wondered, fleetingly, if the dark-haired girl she had noticed behind the wheel of the sports car had been visiting Mr. Trask. If so, why had he frowned just then?

"I'm also very impressed," he went on, "with your project and the preliminary work already done. I think you have a viable proposition."

"Then you will help us?" Kelly asked. "You'll persuade the Society for the Arts to give us their backing?"

"I'll do more than that," Trask replied, smiling broadly. "If they don't agree, I shall finance the project myself."

"Oh, how wonderful!" Kelly almost leaped from her chair. She wanted to rush forward and plant a kiss on the old man's forehead, but stopped herself; he would think her terribly forward. "I can't wait to tell my boss, Mr. Durning."

"Then you will be anxious to return to town," Trask continued. "I'll have Michael show you out."

Kelly rose. She was so excited about his promise that she could hardly think. "Thank you again. It means so much to me. I won't have to continue with the promotion I'm doing now."

"And what is that?"

"Oh, you'll laugh. It's a skydiving promotion; you know, where people actually jump out of airplanes with parachutes!"

He looked at Kelly quizzically. "Skydiving, you say? How odd, coincidental I mean. My son is a skydiver. I keep track of him, although I haven't seen him for years."

Kelly's jaw dropped and she felt slightly queasy.

"He didn't want to come into the Trask business," her host continued, "and left home quite young. I'm afraid we had some rather bitter quarrels, and we haven't spoken in years." He paused again. "He's a very good skydiver, though. You may know him since you're working on a skydiving promotion."

Kelly's voice cracked slightly. "I've only met one so far and his name isn't Trask."

"He hasn't been using my name. He dropped the Trask, whether from desire for anonymity, shame, or fear of embarrassing me, I don't know. He calls himself Steven Barry."

Kelly felt as if the room were spinning, but her thoughts were interrupted by Mr. Trask. "You've never met anyone of that name?" he asked.

Kelly looked into his face, and suddenly the resemblance between the two men became startlingly apparent. The same blue eyes, although the father's were pale and watery now, the same prominent aristocratic nose, the same firm chin that thrust forward, as if daring life to defeat any plans this man would undertake.

"Yes, I know him," she said, her voice barely more than a whisper. Thoughts still whirled in her head.

"I'm glad. He's a wonderful boy, in spite of our differences. He came into my life rather late, you see, and I'm afraid I expected too much of him. When his mother died

. . ." Trask reached out and touched Kelly's hand. "There, there, I mustn't bore you with family history. I hope your promotion is a great success, and I'm looking forward to seeing you again. I shall call you when the funding is all arranged."

"You can reach me at my office. I'd be so grateful." Kelly reached into her bag and pulled out another business card, unable to understand why Steven had sent her here, to his own estranged father. The old man's obvious pain regarding that rift obliterated the happiness she should have felt over his encouragement. In just a short time she had begun to feel very close to Mr. Trask.

She followed the butler back to the front door, climbed into her car, and sped down the driveway, her thoughts in turmoil.

four

When she met Steven at the airport early Saturday morning, Kelly saw that he drove one of the original Thunderbirds, a small dark blue convertible that had been restored with care. She had not intended to let him drive her all the way to Cloverdale, but he insisted that she would get lost otherwise, and besides, it seemed foolish to drive two cars when they were going to the same place.

She settled into the seat beside him, wondering how to broach the subject uppermost in her mind. All week she had pondered Steven's motive in ignoring his father for years, and then suddenly sending her to him. At her taping sessions, reading books into the microphone to record them for blind students, her mind wandered many times to Steven, and she feared her work did not get the attention it deserved. But now the moment had arrived for her to satisfy her curiosity; they would be alone for several hours.

"You look even prettier than usual today," he said, his blue eyes seeming to pierce through her.

Kelly smiled. "Thank you." She smoothed the jacket of her pantsuit into place self-consciously, then tied a matching scarf over her hair. "I met your Mr. Trask," she began.

"I'll bet you liked him and he liked you."

Kelly flashed a look at him. She had not expected this reaction. "As a matter of fact, yes."

"I could predict it; we have similar tastes in women."

"You ought to, since he's your father!" The words came out colder than she had planned.

He glanced quickly at her, then his eyes returned to the road, but his jaw seemed tighter. "So he told you, did he?"

"It came up, yes. I think you intended it to."

"Perhaps."

"In that case, why didn't you tell me yourself?"

After a pause, he said, "I didn't think it was my place. I doubted whether he wanted to acknowledge me as his son, the black sheep and all that."

"What terrible thing did you do that you had to leave home?" Again Kelly regretted her frankness; she was treading where she had no business.

But Steven answered nonetheless. "The unforgivable: I refused to go into the family business."

"I realize your father is elderly, but I didn't think anyone disinherited an unruly son anymore."

Steven opened and closed his mouth twice before answering. "I really don't want to talk about it. Let's change the subject, shall we?"

"I thought you opened the subject by sending me to him."

"Then I made a mistake," he snapped. "I thought I was doing you a favor. I'm sorry, okay?"

Kelly had to admit she stood to gain much and he little, unless he still wanted anxiously to be rid of her. "I'm glad you did, really. I didn't mean to sound ungrateful."

He didn't answer that, and the silence stretched for several miles while Kelly wondered what else she could say to heal the rift. She decided against telling him that on Sunday she had been startled to see Christopher Trask at her church service, sitting in a rear seat. When she tried to find him later to say hello, he had disappeared.

Steven broke the silence. "Did you do your homework?"

"Homework? What homework?"

"Reading about skydiving. Tell me, what's an altimeter?"

Grateful for the end of the uncomfortable interlude, Kelly cleared her throat and attempted an answer. "It's a. . .a gauge, sort of. It tells how high you are off the ground."

"Very good. Not exactly the way I would have phrased it, but acceptable. I'm impressed. What about a rip cord?"

"That's the thing you pull to make the parachute open." Kelly couldn't help smiling with pride at her knowledge, but her pleasure ended when he asked more technical questions for which she was not prepared. He had to answer most of them himself, then explained what would happen at the meet in Cloverdale. Engrossed in all he said, Kelly found the time flew by as fast as the landscape. Before she knew it, they had arrived at their destination.

The town consisted of small stucco houses in pastel colors, but Steven did not stop until they reached the air field well past the residential area. Here, surrounded by distant green and gold hills, a large open meadow, crisscrossed by landing strips, was lined on one side by a set of bleachers. A colorful canopy covered the structure and flags flew from the tops of the small buildings nearby. On the field sat three small planes and one large one.

Spectators arrived, parked their cars in the dirt at the edge of the field, and walked leisurely to the bleachers, where they chose seats for viewing the day's activities. An enterprising vendor hawked his wares—hot dogs and soft drinks—and a young man with a wheeled cart sold ice cream.

Steven and Kelly went directly to the hangar. Several other skydivers stood or sat around, along with an assortment of girlfriends, pilots, mechanics, and some youngsters who were obviously fascinated by anything to do with airplanes.

Having finished her part—the promotion for the event—

Kelly had only to be sure the *Cloverdale Herald* photographer was there taking publicity pictures, and to make sure it all came off as printed in the programs.

The actual event had been planned by one of the many skydiving clubs in California. It consisted of a target contest, where each man would jump from the same altitude and attempt to land on a yellow disc a mere three inches in diameter. The admission charge would benefit the charity which had asked Ingersoll Productions to organize the tour, and the skydivers donated their time and talents. They would have done this on a fine Saturday morning anyway; a victory cup or fancy ribbons constituted their prizes.

Kelly took in the sights and sounds of the sport. The talk seemed almost exclusively concerned with wind conditions, which she didn't understand. All of the men—there were no women skydivers present this particular day—wore colorful jumpsuits made of a nylon-like material. They fit closely at neck, wrists, and ankles and contained numerous zippered pockets. Heavy-looking black boots and plastic helmets completed the costume. A row of parachutes rested on a large table in the corner, with more parachutes on the floor nearby. Someone had brought a large pot of coffee, and all helped themselves to it, using Styrofoam cups. No one ate, however, although it was past noon, and Kelly's stomach was beginning to protest the absence of food.

Steven pulled an orange jumpsuit over his street clothes and changed from scruffy tennis shoes to his own black boots. Then he came back to where Kelly waited and introduced her to the others. She knew she wouldn't remember all their names, but she tried to make mental notes of who they were from some identifiable feature. In their jumpsuits and helmets, however, they all tended to look alike.

"This is Gary Nelson," Steven said. "He's the president of the Cloverdale Skydiving Club."

"How do you do?" Kelly said, and shook hands with the tall, thin young man whose brown hair waved back from a high forehead.

"Glad to meet you," he said, squeezing Kelly's hand in a firm grip. "I hear you're the P.R. person for this whole tour of Steven's. Sounds like a mighty responsible job. And you seem to have done well today; there are certainly a lot more people here than I expected."

"Thanks. We hope to raise a large amount for charity."

"Well, excuse me, Miss Marsh, I have a few more things to do. Starting time is one o'clock," and he walked away.

"Find a good seat where you can watch," Steven said.

"I suppose I should, but first I think I'll patronize that vendor and get something to eat—I'm famished. Aren't you going to eat something too?"

"No, most skydivers don't eat just before jumping."

"I once read that bullfighters don't eat beforehand just in case they're gored and have to have a quick operation."

Steven's face took on a puzzled look, and he waited a moment before answering. "You read too much," he said stiffly.

"I beg your pardon."

"There's very little similarity between skydiving and bull-fighting. We have no adversary up there except ourselves, and if an accident occurs, no surgeon in the world will be able to put us back together again, lunch or not."

"I'm sorry," Kelly stammered. "I didn't mean—"

"It's all right. I know what you meant. It's what we love to do and we don't think it's dangerous—although sometimes we like the public to think it is—but we never lose sight of the fact that stupidity and carelessness can cause accidents. Maybe we don't eat before a jump because we're nervous."

"No one looks nervous. You all look so completely relaxed and carefree."

"Oh, we're nervous all right—but don't tell anyone I said that." He smiled and gave her a wink.

Kelly suddenly lost her hunger, and she too became nervous: for him, for all the men who were going to defy death this afternoon with only a piece of nylon for protection.

"I'm beginning to think I shouldn't have come along after all," she said, frowning, "I couldn't take it if someone, someone. . ." She couldn't finish the sentence.

"Hey, wait a minute," Steven said, taking her hand. "Don't even think it! Nothing's going to happen. Being nervous is just part of the routine. It happens to everyone in sports: the downhill skier just before he pushes off, or the race-car driver in the pit before the flag drops. That's what it's all about!"

"But this is dangerous. What if the chute doesn't open?"

"The chances of a parachute not opening are about one in ten thousand. And we wear two of them, remember? What do you suppose the chances are of both of them not opening?"

"Pretty high, I guess."

"Right. Besides that, we all pack our own. And professional packers do the reserve chute. That raises the odds too. Furthermore, someone once fell out of a plane with *no* parachute at all and lived to talk about it."

"I see." Kelly tried to feel reassured, and the touch of his hand comforted her, but as the tension mounted in the hangar as the men began to put on their chutes, she found she couldn't erase the flutterings inside her body.

"Go on out now," Steven urged, fastening on a parachute.

Kelly followed another girl to a ladder at the side of a building and climbed to the flat roof which gave a view of the field, its target circle, and the plane taxiing to the runway. In a few moments the boys who had been in the hangar and some of the girlfriends of other skydivers joined her.

The hot afternoon sun beat down as they watched the converted C-47 getting into position, a door on one side conveniently removed. Then the twelve skydivers walked out to the field, to the shouts and applause of the crowd, and entered the plane. It roared off into the cloudless sky. A hush fell over everyone; even the vendors stopped their calls of "Buy your popcorn here."

Necks craning, heads tilted upward, all watched the aircraft become the size of a toy plane against the blue backdrop of the sky. Then someone called, "Here he comes," and Kelly saw the first man leap from the open door of the plane and come falling to earth, arms and legs spread out and slightly bent at elbows and knees. He fell for what seemed an incredibly long time, his figure easily discernible by the time he pulled his rip cord and the parachute billowed out above him, snapping him upward into a perpendicular position.

Then began the test of his skill, maneuvering his chute in the air. The parachutes the men used today were not round, but rectangular in shape, like quilted bed sheets in the wind, Kelly thought. Lower and lower he came, and finally he touched down near the target, not directly on it, but close. Three striped-shirted judges announced his distance at only six centimeters. The crowd roared its approval, and the skydiver, pulling his chute down, hastily got out of the way of the next man, who was already close to the pit.

Several jumpers touched the edges of the disc, which seemed as close as anyone could come, but Kelly knew Steven's reputation as the best, and she had already seen him land right on a similar target less than a week before.

Steven was the last man out of the plane, and her pulse began to race as soon as she saw him in the air. Her neck aching from the strain of looking up, she watched him free-fall, arms and legs outstretched, his jumpsuit vivid against the sky around him, the darker color of the parachutes on his chest and back giving him a distorted outline.

Pull the rip cord, she told him mentally. *You're too low; pull your rip cord!* Seconds stretched into minutes in her mind, and her entire body seemed bathed in perspiration. She thought she would burst from the tension. Then the chute popped out, and she watched him pull on the lines and make the chute go sideways in the sky, his head down, concentrating on the target below.

One foot raised and bent at the knee, the other landed dead center on the disc, driving it into the ground. The crowd screamed; people jumped up and down in the stands. Kelly breathed again. *He's safe,* she thought; *he's safe.*

And then a terrible thought came to her. *I've been worried. But he's done this dozens—maybe hundreds—of times before. He was never in any real danger. Why do I care? Am I falling in love with him?* She sat still, unheeding of the others around her. *I can't be,* she told herself. *I can't be falling in love with a skydiver. And certainly not with that one.*

She had always felt content with her life, her career, her church, her volunteer work. In due time a man might come along who shared her beliefs: a reliable, caring, and unselfish man, above all a Christian. But skydivers! Their hedonistic lifestyle, hanging around airports, jumping out of planes, contributed little to society. Until *she* had come along and put them to work for charity!

As for Steven, he might be the worst of the lot. He had left a fine home and family business, saddened his father, lived the life of an irresponsible gypsy, attracting crowds of impressionable young girls. True, he could be charming when it suited him; he had apologized for his bad manners and been very informative and pleasant on the drive down— but he was so unpredictable. One moment he seemed maddeningly belligerent, and the next he kissed her impetuously.

Well, she asked herself, *which is it you most object to: his male chauvinism or his personal attentions?*

Try as she would, she couldn't stop thinking of the way his lips felt on hers, the bold way he held her, just like he treated the parachute and made it do as he wished. She had never wanted a conquering type of man; she didn't want one now. She absolutely refused to fall in love with Steven Barry.

That settled, she came down from her perch and bought a hot dog and popcorn.

five

The plane went up again and again, each man having six jumps that afternoon; their total score would indicate the winner. Whereas none of the men, except Steven, had hit the disc dead center on the first try, they improved with practice, and all of them did it by the third jump. Gary Nelson, whom Kelly remembered meeting in the hangar, hit dead center on the second and every other jump until the sixth, and then missed it by four centimeters, the same as he had the first time.

Steven, with five dead center landings, was thus assured of winning, so long as he landed no farther than seven centimeters on the last try. But this time his approach seemed off, as if he were tired, and Kelly became tense, hoping he'd make it but afraid he would miss by just enough to lose the contest. But then, in the last split seconds, he maneuvered the parachute over the pit area, and his foot went down almost on top of the disc, a mere three centimeters off. He had won the event.

The men lined up on the judges' platform, and the prizes were awarded, accompanied by loud applause from the audience.

A noisy, happy crowd filled the small cafe where they all assembled for dinner that night. Huge platters of spaghetti, bowls of salad, and baskets of Italian bread covered the red cloth-covered tables. There were almost thirty people in the group, half of them young girls who looked up adoringly at their skydiver boyfriends and hung on their every word.

Kelly sat between Steven and Gary and listened to the banter between them about coming in first and second again. Gary vowed he would beat Steven at it one day, and they talked about their jumps, how the wind affected them, and many things about parachutes which Kelly didn't understand.

Other events, other days, other people, were spoken of all around her, and Kelly found, surprisingly, the talk interesting, even exciting, though she could not participate. Gary politely asked her about her promotion work and seemed interested in hearing about advertising copyrighting and layouts. To Kelly it had become suddenly terribly boring. Previously she had only compared her job with the office work of her friends, and in that context hers was far more varied—but it could hardly compare to skydiving for excitement.

Steven tried to include her in the conversation, but content to listen, she watched him, unable to help admiring his handsome profile, the way his dark hair grew low on his neck.

It was almost midnight when they finally tore themselves away from the camaraderie of the cafe and headed back toward the cars, the couples pairing off, arms about each other's waists. Kelly felt self-conscious and wondered if anyone thought she and Steven were pairing off for the night, but she said nothing. She followed him to the convertible, and they roared off down the open highway.

"How did you like your first parachuting event?"

"I loved it," Kelly admitted. "I had no idea it would be so exciting and yet so. . .so controlled. Of course, you told me in advance about the competition and the judges and all that, but somehow, seeing it firsthand is very different."

"Are you ready to admit we're not a bunch of crack-pots?"

"I suppose so. After seeing you and the others jump so often in one afternoon, I've almost begun to take it for granted."

"I told you it was safe."

"Safe? Hardly that," Kelly denied.

"There's an old joke that goes, 'What's the most danger-ous part of skydiving?' and the answer is, 'Driving to the airport!'"

Kelly laughed with him. "Even when I became accus-tomed to it," she added, "I still had a scary feeling when I saw you jump from the plane and you seemed to float in the air. Even though I knew you'd open your parachute, there was a moment. . ."

"When you were worried about me?"

Kelly flushed, glad of the darkness that kept him from seeing her face. "I didn't mean you personally," she amended. "I meant any of the men." She couldn't admit to him that indeed he, personally, concerned her, and she had begun to think about him even when he was not in midair.

"What about you? What do you feel?" she went on. "Is it always exciting? Is that why you do it so much?"

"Yes, it's always exciting. . .at least. . ." Kelly wondered if he considered the danger, even though he might not con-sciously admit it, but he didn't finish his sentence.

"What do you do when you're not jumping?" she asked. "Just wait around impatiently for the next weekend?"

"Hardly. I have to work; skydiving is not the cheapest sport in the world. I teach both skydiving and flying, and I take people up for airplane rides, things like that."

"Then you do spend all of your time there, your own little world, as it were?"

"You make it sound provincial," he said lightly. "I assure you I know what's going on in the world. My entire being isn't centered on the distance between plane and earth."

"Still, you are somewhat. . .isolated, aren't you, from what happens in the real world?"

"That depends on what you mean by 'real,' doesn't it?"

"I don't mean to insult you," Kelly added. "Please don't take it that way. I'm only trying to understand what fascinates you so that you spend your entire life—"

"Some people," Steven answered, cutting her off, "would think my father's world is real, running Trask Enterprises from behind a desk. I couldn't spend my entire life doing *that*."

Kelly paused before replying. "Many people manage a normal career and hobbies at the same time."

He turned toward her, stared at her face for a few seconds. "I'd rather not talk about it. I have no intention of justifying my existence to you, at least not tonight."

"Well," Kelly said, "I seem to have a knack for bringing up subjects you can't discuss."

Steven lifted his right hand from the steering wheel and covered Kelly's where it lay on the seat between them. The warm, strong touch sent a tingle through her.

"It's not your fault," he said. "It's mine."

"No, you were quite right. Your lifestyle is your own affair; I shouldn't have pried."

"Your curiosity is normal—in fact, flattering. And as you said earlier today, I rather invited it by telling you about my father. I think I've wanted to confide in you, to get to know you well, since the moment we met."

He squeezed her hand, then Kelly pulled it away. If he were hinting that something could develop between them, she would have to discourage him immediately. She had already decided her future could not possibly include a skydiver.

"I think it's time we did change the subject," she said, trying to make her inflection light and breezy. "We could talk about the weather. Oh, excuse me," she gave a little laugh, "that would be shop talk for you, wouldn't it? Well, then, how about books or music or the theater?"

"That's your field, isn't it?" he asked, his voice equally bantering. "You'd no doubt put me at a disadvantage. Instead—"

But he never got to finish his thought because suddenly the car made a strange noise and smoke began to pour from the hood. He pulled the Thunderbird over to the side of the road and turned off the engine, then got out and raised the hood. After several minutes, he opened his door and climbed back in beside her.

"What's the matter?" she asked. "Is something wrong with the car? Can you fix it?" Being stranded on a deserted road in the middle of the proverbial nowhere held no appeal.

"Yes, something is definitely wrong with the car, and yes, I can fix it; the problem is I can't fix it tonight. I'm going to need some daylight. Also, I'm much too tired to tackle it now."

He got out of the car again and went around to the trunk where he kept his parachutes, only this time he pulled out a sleeping bag. "I think it's 'sleeping under the stars' time."

"But you can't!" she protested. "What am I supposed to do while you're sleeping in some meadow?"

"Join me, of course. I have two sleeping bags."

"I can't possibly do that." She got out of the car nevertheless and joined him at its rear. "Isn't there some other alternative?"

He had the second sleeping bag out now and hefted one under each arm. "There may be a motel nearby, but I honestly don't know where, maybe miles away. Or we could stand here with our thumbs out and hope to hitch a ride. Frankly, I don't think this road is heavily traveled. Believe me, sleeping out is less trouble."

"But I can't."

"You mean you never have. Come on," he urged, "can't you be a little unconventional, just once?"

He was so jolly, so pleased with his solution to the problem, that Kelly's anger fizzled. Besides, the night was warm and balmy—and many of her friends camped out frequently in tents or sleeping bags. She relaxed. It might be an interesting adventure.

Steven had started off across the field at the side of the road, a hayfield apparently. He called back to her, "Look, that's just what we want." He ran to where a few bundles of hay lay. They were poor leftovers, puny, imperfectly baled. "Can you pick up that small one?"

Kelly tried to lift one end of the bale, but instead some straw broke off in her hand and sent her tumbling backward.

Steven burst into laughter and so did she, realizing how funny she must look, sitting in the field, bits of hay all over her clothes and in her hair.

"Never mind," Steven said. "I'll do it; you get the two sleeping bags." He dragged the reluctant bale to the shelter of a clump of trees.

When she reached his side, pulling a sleeping bag in each hand, he was sniffing the air. "Skunks," he said.

Kelly moved closer to him, looked around apprehensively. "How do you know?"

"Don't tell me you've never smelled a skunk before?"

"I think I've smelled that odor before, but I didn't know it was a skunk."

"My dear young lady," he said, in mock seriousness, "you may know all there is about music, books, and drama, but it's time you learned something about the *real* world." Then he laughed, and she joined in.

"But is it safe here with skunks around?"

"Oh, they aren't here now; they're more scared of us." He began to pull straw out of the bale and spread it on the ground. "If we unzip both bags," he suggested, "we can spread one out on the straw for a mattress, and then put the other over us as a blanket."

"Oh, no, you don't," Kelly said hastily, snatching up one of the bags from him. "We'll sleep separately, if you don't mind."

"I'm only trying to help," he said, pretending to be wounded by her assumptions. "It would be warmer that way."

"I don't think we need to be concerned about warmth." She smiled nevertheless, amused by his playfulness. "In fact, it's far too warm for sleeping bags," and with that she opened hers flat after all, slipped off her jacket and sandals, and lay down without any covering, savoring the balmy air that touched her face and arms.

Steven spread his sleeping bag nearby, and Kelly, aware of his presence next to her, did not feel tired anymore. Her blood seemed to be racing in her veins, and sleep was the furthest thing from her mind. She closed her eyes tightly to squeeze out even the peripheral sight of him, but they refused to stay shut, springing open as if defying her will.

She stared up at the sky, immediately enraptured with the deep blackness of the night and the millions of stars, so bright they seemed near enough to touch. She forgot Steven momentarily in exploring the heavens, searching for the constellations she remembered from her school days. Why, there was the Big Dipper.

Suddenly his warm breath brushed her cheek. "It's beautiful, isn't it?" he asked in a soft, low voice.

"Yes, it is." She remembered something appropriate.

"The day Thou gavest, Lord, is ended,
  The darkness fades at Thy behest.
To thee our morning hymns ascended,
  Thy praise shall sanctify our rest."

"That's from a hymn, isn't it?" Steven asked.

"Yes, how did you know?"

"My mother used to sing it to me." His eyes were closed, his voice almost inaudible, as if he were reliving the past.

"And you remembered. You surprise me."

His eyes opened, and he looked at her with a smile. "It surprises you that I'm not an uncultured lout? You've enjoyed thinking of me that way, haven't you?"

"You never contradicted me," she countered.

He laughed gently, the sound too light to disturb the quiet of their mood. "I played a game; I often do, you know. It amused me to let you think the worst of me."

"And now?"

"And now I want to play a different role. I don't want you to see me as the. . .daredevil I sometimes pretend to be."

"Must you always pretend?" Kelly asked.

"I'm not now."

Kelly didn't dare look at him, for the tension that had momentarily abated in her delight at the wonders of the sky now returned in full force. Every muscle seemed suddenly vibrant and alive, tingling with sensation.

She heard him move and flashed a look at him, affirming what she suspected: he was raised on one elbow, staring into her face, only inches away. Her voice choked and she could only say hoarsely, "Steven, no."

Ignoring her feeble protest, his lips came down on hers. The kiss was soft as a flower petal, and Kelly could not move a muscle. He raised his face again, looking intently into her eyes. She lay still, waiting—yes, waiting, she forced herself to admit—for him to kiss her again.

As if in complete understanding, his lips, before so tender and swift, came this time firm with pressure. Her arms went instinctively around his neck, and she felt as if every nerve ending was alive with sensation. His lips left hers, and he kissed her cheeks, her eyelids. His husky voice left soft, indistinguishable words in her hair.

Then, like a bubble bursting, Kelly's ecstacy evaporated. Her throat tightened and cold reality came flooding in on her. Why had she let him kiss her, this man whom she had disliked scant weeks ago, who even now she would never consciously choose for herself?

She pulled her arms from his neck and pushed against his chest. He looked into her face, questioning her sudden withdrawal.

"Please stop," she said through dry and trembling lips.

"I'm only—"

"You were only trying to make love to me," she said, struggling from his embrace.

"You seemed to enjoy it."

"You're playing another game," she retorted, remembering his earlier words. "Well, this is one game I don't play."

"No," he answered, "you don't understand."

Not listening, angry at her own betraying emotions, she lashed out at him. "Don't lie to me. You wanted to make love to me, so you could add another conquest to your list. Well, I won't be one of your groupies!"

She tried to rise from the makeshift bed, but Steven, now sitting upright, shoved her back down on the sleeping bag.

"Lie still," he demanded, "and listen to me. Yes, I kissed you. Yes, I enjoyed it. And I also admit being caught up in the moment. So were you, by the way," he accused.

He paused and his eyes seemed to glow like cat's eyes in the dark. "I never planned to make love to you, certainly not against your will. I don't need a string of conquests to prove anything. I know who and what I am. And I suggest you might think about that yourself. You were far from an unwilling participant a moment ago. You'd better make up your mind exactly how you feel before you accuse me of having designs on your body. In other words, Miss Marsh, reserve your maidenly protests for when you're asked!"

With that he snatched his sleeping bag from her side and moved it to the far edge of the straw, then threw himself on it and turned his back to her.

Kelly stared at his withdrawn form, feeling shattered, confused, humiliated, and ashamed. After a moment, she got to her feet and carried the sleeping bag back to the car.

The interior of the Thunderbird was too cramped for her to lie down. She huddled on the seat for what seemed hours, staring up through the windshield into the sky, feeling like a complete fool. He was right, of course; she shouldn't have assumed he was trying to make love to her. And if he had been, hadn't she invited it by her own actions? She knew better than to spend the night lying so close to a man; to do so was simply asking for trouble. But he was so—

she might as well admit it, at least to herself—so physically attractive, so glamorous. She, who never allowed herself to be taken in by such qualities, had succumbed, like a child in a candy store. Hot tears escaped from under her eyelids and slid across her cheeks.

Gradually she calmed down. She rolled down the window and listened to the sounds of crickets and night birds. Her head fell back against the seat, and her eyes closed, but she still heard questions running through her head. *What's happening to me? Why am I unable to think clearly when I'm near him?*

There was no answer, but knowing the danger, she would never let it happen again. They still had five more promotions to do together, so she made herself a promise. She would never be alone with him again.

She drifted into sleep, and in her dreams she saw a dark-haired man, who looked very much like Steven Barry, come up the walk of a vine-covered cottage. He wore a jumpsuit over business clothes, and a helmet shone on his head. Not a skydiving helmet, but a silver visored one, the kind worn by knights!

⁂

Kelly thought she must still be dreaming when the first sound to come to her ears was a noisy pounding. She sat up straighter in the car seat and looked around. The Thunderbird's hood was up, and through the crack between the hood and the windshield, she could see a figure bent over the engine. Steven.

She opened the car door and got out stiffly. Steven turned his head and acknowledged her. "Good morning, sleepyhead. I'm onto your tactics, you know. You were just pretending to be asleep so you could avoid helping me fix this ancient heap of mine. Well, you won. It's done now." He slammed down the hood.

Kelly could hardly believe her ears. He was so cheerful, as if their words of the night before were never spoken. Nevertheless, she didn't know what to say. She gave him a weak smile, and he took the sleeping bag from her and stowed it in the trunk.

He held her door and when she was seated, he got into the driver's seat and started the engine. It hummed fairly normally, Kelly thought.

"It's put together with wire and a prayer, but it'll last until we get back to civilization."

Again Kelly remained silent, but as they headed for the city again, Steven kept up the small talk. "You seem to have slept like a baby, even if you must have been a little cramped."

Kelly wondered why he remained so cheerful. Did it mean his anger was completely gone? Perhaps she should apologize anyway. "About last night—" she began, but he cut her short.

"Last night was a mistake. But I didn't plan it."

"I know you didn't. We were both. . .I shouldn't have accused you. . ."

"The truth is you *should* accuse me. If you were any other woman, I probably *would* have tried to make love to you, but with you. . ."

"We haven't known each other very long," she offered.

"It's not that. There's something else about you. I felt it from the first—that's what upset me. I'm afraid too many women have flung themselves at me. But you were different, and I wanted to break down your resistance. Or else make you angry."

"But you said—"

"When I got to know you better, I realized I could never

take advantage of you—but I couldn't help wanting to kiss you last night. I guess what I'm trying to say is that I'd like us to be—not lovers, not yet—but more than friends."

He placed his arm around her shoulders and pulled her to his side. Her thoughts were confused; suddenly she felt like she was sixteen again and having her first date with a boy. But teenage dates were just that, and they didn't mean anything; they were not commitments for the future. If she accepted Steven's attentions, he might think she could be serious about him, and she couldn't. She was no teenager and her life plan did not include this type of man. It would be cruel to lead him on.

She remembered her promise to herself of the night before, how confident she had felt that she could continue to do her job, work with him as long as necessary, and still not become involved with him. But how could she tell him without antagonizing him, perhaps jeopardizing the harmony of the program?

"Let's stop for breakfast somewhere. I'm famished," he said.

She glanced at her watch. "Steven, I can't. It's Sunday morning. I have to go to church."

"Church?" His gaze turned to her briefly, then back to the road, and he removed his arm from her shoulder and grunted, "Well, okay."

"You could go with me."

"Thanks. Some other time, perhaps."

"Steven, there's something you need to know about me. I've tried to tell you, but perhaps I've been too subtle. I'm a Christian."

"I know that."

"I work at it. And. . ." she struggled to find just the right words, ". . . We can't ever be anything to one another unless you're a Christian too." She paused to let that register. "I hope we *can* be friends, but—"

"Okay, okay," he interrupted. "I get it." His face showed strain, and his lips were a tight thin line. Then, finally, he turned to her and said in a softer voice, "I'm sorry I overstepped the bounds. But it's okay. It's good we both know where we stand. No hard feelings."

He turned on the car radio and listened in silence, wrapped in his own thoughts apparently, so Kelly was spared the necessity of doing any more explaining. Almost before she knew it, the trip ended.

Back at the airport in town, where she had left her own car the previous day, Kelly saw several people on the field already, in spite of the time and the day. She had hoped for a few moments of privacy with Steven, unhindered by his driving, but as the Thunderbird pulled into the parking lot and they alighted, Red Johnson approached.

"Hey, where have you two been?" Red grinned like a conspirator and punched a friendly fist into Steven's side.

"Lay off," Steven said, and Kelly felt her scalp tingle with embarrassment. Naturally they were all assuming she and Steven had spent the night together—and not as innocently as it had turned out. But she knew that trying to explain would only make it seem worse, so she remained silent.

"I think I'll be going now," she said quietly.

"I'll see you tomorrow." Steven held her hand for a brief moment as they walked toward her small compact. Then she got in, and after closing the door for her, he walked away.

Kelly started the car and slowly backed it out of its parking place, then maneuvered it through the lot toward the exit. Through the rearview mirror, she noticed Steven was not walking back to his own car. Instead, he headed toward a tall, dark-haired girl. The distance between them did nothing to hide the fact that she wore brilliantly red lipstick, her black hair flowed glamorously around her shoulders, and a bright green dress emphasized her stunning figure.

Kelly's car slowed to a stop, as she unconsciously lifted her foot from the accelerator and stared at the girl, who looked somehow familiar. Where had she seen that face before?

The girl threw her arms around Steven's neck and they hugged; then she led him to a small red sports car.

And then it occurred to Kelly where she had seen that face; it was on the way to the Trask house almost a week ago. The girl had been driving that red sports car on the wrong side of the road, forcing Kelly to swerve into the grass.

Kelly's foot came down hard, and her car leaped forward like a jackrabbit. As she swerved into the street, tears stung her eyes. So, all his talk about their becoming more than friends had been just another line. It was obvious he already had a lover, one of those teenagers, no doubt, who would do anything for a skydiver.

Stomach churning, breathing labored, Kelly struggled to compose herself as she drove. Why had this upset her so? She did not want the man herself, so why the anger? She told herself it was the deception. Why had he tried to deceive her?

She calmed down and forced herself to think rationally. She did not want him for a husband; therefore, she had no right to care how he conducted his life. Their relationship was strictly a business one, and the appearance of the beautiful brunette would actually simplify her task of keeping

Steven in his place. She should be grateful, actually, that this had happened. It protected her from falling in love with the wrong man.

But why did she feel so disappointed, so desolate?

six

Kelly had calmed down considerably on Monday, yet she still felt a nagging pain in the pit of her stomach at the prospect of confronting Steven when she returned to the airport.

She spent the morning in her office, making telephone calls, writing news releases, and preparing sketches for posters for the upcoming exhibitions. By noon, she realized she had been postponing the inevitable and headed for Flyway Aviation; once there, however, she rationalized that she couldn't do any work on an empty stomach and decided to have lunch in the wood-framed building that served as the field's only restaurant.

Finding Red Johnson alone at a table, she joined him. He jumped up at her approach and held a chair for her.

"Thank you," she said, smiling. "You're a real gentleman. It's seldom I have my chair held for me anymore."

"I guess I just can't stop doing things the old way," he said, returning her smile. "No matter what the women's lib types think, I still like to treat women with respect. Especially pretty ones like yourself," he added with a wink.

"Well, thank you again," Kelly said.

"I may not be young anymore," he said, "but I still appreciate the finer things in life."

"You're not old, Red," Kelly insisted.

"Sure, the Rocky Mountains got a few years on me, but I got *shoes* that are older than you are! This hair used to be red," he said, pointing to his head.

Kelly disagreed. "It's still red."

"Nope, now it's so full of gray, people think it's blond. Or worse, 'strawberry'!" He scowled at the thought, then grinned again, as if laughing at his own predicament.

They ordered lunch, and while waiting for it to be served, Kelly asked Red if he had looked over her final plans for the drops. They had agreed in advance that she would make the plans but he would double-check, since she wasn't as familiar with the procedures. Today, she was especially grateful for this arrangement, as it meant she might not have to see Steven at all. She didn't know how she'd react to him, or he to her, after their experience on the weekend.

"Yes," Red assured her. "You did just fine. Got the right type of plane and some good pilots. You even got all those pesky forms signed okay."

"That's the worst part," Kelly said. "I had no idea authorities required so much paperwork before they'd let someone do sport parachuting."

"Gets worse every year," Red said. "And you know, every year more and more people do it, and it keeps getting safer and more common, and yet every year someone else seems to get into the act and require another form. Why, I remember when all I had to do was get permission from the pilot!"

"Did you used to jump, Red? I didn't know that."

"Yes, I was one of the first. Would you believe it? That was almost forty years ago."

"I had no idea people had been doing it that long."

"Longer than that. Parachutes are older than airplanes."

"You're not serious?" Kelly scoffed.

"Seventeen ninety-seven!" he said triumphantly. "They used to jump from air balloons."

"But you said you're one of the first. Come on now,

you're not *that* old."

They both laughed, and then the waitress brought their food. When she left, Red continued, although he alternated talking and taking bites of his thick ham and swiss cheese sandwich. "I meant in the United States," he said. "The sport started in France, and I learned from a Frenchman myself."

"You don't mean Jacques Istel, do you?" Kelly asked.

Red paused, his sandwich halfway to his mouth. "You know about Istel?"

"I came across his name in my reading."

"I learned from another fellow, Georges something or other. Can you believe it? I've forgotten his last name. But I met Jacques Istel once. I lived in Phoenix—it was '61 or '62—and he came there to do a jump. Didn't look like a Frenchman to me. Too tall, I thought, where Georges was shorter with dark hair."

"Did you jump with Istel?"

"Nope. He ran his own show." He paused as if reminiscing.

"I'll bet you've seen a lot of interesting things."

"Yes, the sport sure has changed over the years. Why, I remember when they had free-fall contests to see how long you could fall before you opened your parachute, nothing any sane person would do today."

"Why is that?"

"Well, how long you fall depends on your altitude when you jump, doesn't it?"

"I guess so."

"And we all jumped from the same plane and it went up to the same height."

"I see. You mean in order to win the contest you had to delay opening the parachute as long as possible."

"Risk your neck, come close to killing yourself!"

Kelly was shocked at the thought of men seeing how close they could come to the ground before opening the parachute, like teenagers daring one another playing "chicken" with automobiles on back roads. "Didn't someone stop it?"

"Oh, sure, the skydivers themselves. They regulated things and made safety rules, and they just stopped having contests like that. These days they do more landing on targets. I remember when the targets were just large strips of white cloth laid on the ground in the shape of an X. Now the jumpers are so accurate they land on that little disc. And they have competitions to do certain stunts in the air, and make stars, like they're going to do at the lake. It's all a lot safer. I hate all the paperwork, but I'm sure glad they made some rules."

"So am I. I couldn't possibly be involved with anything like that. In fact, I almost didn't take this assignment because I thought the sport was too dangerous."

"Like I've just been saying, it's not anymore. You ought to try it yourself."

"Try skydiving?" Kelly asked.

"Sure, why not?"

"Don't people still get killed?"

"A lot more people get killed driving cars, but that doesn't stop anyone from doing it. Same with skydiving. Besides, if you're one of the sensible ones, it's perfectly safe. More people get hurt in their bathrooms and kitchens than anywhere else."

"That's an interesting statistic," Kelly admitted, "but even if I believed it to be the safest sport in the world, I. . ." She paused in mid-sentence. Red continued drinking his coffee and didn't press her to go on.

Kelly had always been an honest person, even to herself, and she had to admit that she had begun to have an interest in the sport. Spending so much time at the field, watching so many jumps, it had begun to fascinate her. Although she didn't think she wanted to do it herself, she was beginning to understand why others might.

"I really don't think I want to jump," she finished.

"You don't have to do an actual jump," Red answered. "You could just take the ground lessons. It would give you a good idea of the kind of training a jumper gets before he goes up for the first time. It could even help you with your job here. It never hurts to know as much as possible about something you're connected with."

Kelly knew Red was right about that; she had always believed in getting all the facts.

"I suppose I could do that," she said. "What's it like, a lot of lectures? How can you practice something you have to get right the first time?"

Red grinned. "Oh, you'd be surprised what you'd learn." Then he added eagerly, "There's a class starting tomorrow. It goes for three days. You just take those and you'll learn plenty. I guarantee you'll be a different woman."

Kelly looked skeptically at her red-headed friend. "I'm not sure I want to be a different woman, but I'll think about it. Where does one sign up?"

"You don't have to sign up. Just come to the office tomorrow afternoon at two o'clock. Wear a jumpsuit—you can buy new or secondhand equipment at the store on the other side of the field you know—and I'll give you a book to read first."

"I'll read the book, but I can't promise the other."

"Believe me, it's not like the old days. Sometimes I wonder how I stayed alive, jumping all those years ago, when they didn't have licensed instructors or jumpmasters or supervised competitions."

"What's a jumpmaster?" Kelly asked.

"The person in charge of every jump, just like it sounds. He's the boss, and no one does anything except what the jumpmaster tells him."

"Is Steven a jumpmaster?" Kelly asked, then wished she had not brought up his name. She didn't want Red—or anyone—to realize the man occupied so much of her thoughts.

"Oh, yes," Red said. "He's an instructor and jumpmaster and best at both. He won second place in international competition. And in two years when they hold it again, he'll probably come in first. But I remember when he first started. He was a wild one."

"You've known Steven a long time then?" Kelly asked.

"Longer than anyone except his folks, I guess. He never talks about them, but I understand his mother died when he was young. Once Steven let things slip, and I figured out his father wanted him to go into the family business. When Steven wouldn't, the old man never forgave him. They never see each other now."

"How sad," Kelly said, remembering her visit with Mr. Trask.

"He's a strange one, that Steven," Red added. "He lets me father him a little—give him some advice—but otherwise he's pretty much of a loner. Oh, he has girlfriends," he added, a twinkle coming into his eyes. "Maybe I'd better warn you—don't lose your head over him. He breaks hearts as often as you put gas in your car!"

Kelly blushed against her will. "Oh, I won't lose my head," she said hastily. "I have no plans to fall in love with anyone right now, much less someone who makes his living leaping out of airplanes!"

"Mind you," Red continued, "I love that boy. I think he's one of the best there is. But he's not ready to settle down yet. It's like he's waiting for something—I can't figure out what—but when it comes, well, he'll probably make a good husband. He does everything the best he can, puts his whole heart and soul in it. I think he'd be that way with a wife too, once he makes up his mind to it."

Kelly grudgingly admitted to herself that Red undoubtedly knew Steven much better than she, but Steven's possible qualifications as a husband held no interest for her, even if true. He was still not the man for her.

"And Steven is the strictest about the rules, too."

"Who's strictest about rules?" The deep voice of Steven himself interrupted the conversation, and Kelly felt a stirring deep inside as she saw his dark good looks. "May I join you?" he asked. "I'd like to hear more about this strict person." His infectious grin brought a smile to Kelly's lips in spite of herself.

Red urged Steven to sit down. "You know I'm talking about you."

The waitress came over and Steven ordered, then turned back to Red. "I don't think of my attitude as strict, just firm. But I don't want to discuss myself." He turned to face Kelly.

"We were talking about the old days, too," Red added.

"And what old stories did you dredge up to amuse Kelly?"

"I was going to tell her about the accident in Mendoza."

Steven's smile disappeared at once and a frown took its place. "That's not a pleasant story. Why don't you forget it?"

Kelly sensed she would learn something more about Steven's personality, and she turned to Red. "I'd like to know everything about skydiving. Please tell me."

Red looked at Steven from the corners of his eyes, but slowly began the tale. "It was a long time ago—ten years maybe—when Joe Paddroni killed himself—"

Steven sounded bitter. "He didn't kill himself. You make it sound like suicide. It was an accident."

"That's what *we* said," Red argued, "but you. . ."

In silence, the two men looked at each other. Kelly felt they each remembered something different about the incident, and she had an overpowering desire to hear the complete story.

"What happened?" she asked.

Red continued slowly, his voice barely audible. "Steven was the first to reach Joe, and he snatched off his parachute, got in the plane, and jumped with it."

Kelly's voice was a whisper. "He jumped with the dead man's parachute?"

"Yep, bloody and everything. We would have stopped him, but we didn't realize what he planned to do until he went up. He had just jumped himself and wasn't wearing an emergency chute."

"Kelly doesn't want to hear this," Steven snapped. "I was only a kid then, a stupid kid. Let's forget it."

"You said you had to do it."

Steven took over the story, although he seemed to be talking to himself, his head lowered. "Of course I thought I had to do it. I was full of dumb ideas in those days."

"Why would you do that?"

"I thought I had to prove something. I barely knew Joe, but I thought I knew parachutes. I didn't think the parachute had failed. I thought he hadn't pulled the rip cord."

Kelly visualized a youthful Steven snatching up the dead man's parachute and jumping with it. How typical of him, impetuous and overconfident. She spoke softly. "So you jumped with it, and pulled the rip cord, and. . .it worked! You were right."

"Or I wouldn't be here today, would I?" Steven's head came up and he added, "I told you we shouldn't talk about that."

Red nodded. "You said you didn't want parachuting to get a bad name."

At that Steven burst into a loud laugh. "I don't remember *that*!"

Kelly thought she knew what Steven remembered about the incident, that if he hadn't jumped with the parachute, everyone would have gone on thinking of it as an accident. But when it worked, it could only mean that Joe hadn't pulled the rip cord. Had the man wanted to die, or had he just panicked somehow?

She shivered, then brought her thoughts back to the conversation in time to catch Red saying, "As a matter of fact, we were just arranging for Kelly to take lessons."

Kelly flashed a warning look at the older man, but it was too late. He went blithely on, telling Steven all about their discussion and that Kelly had just agreed to take three ground school lessons. Her skin tingling, she wished she could close Red's mouth. Why did Steven have to know? He would think her decision stemmed from an interest in him, and she would have a harder time keeping her distance from him. "I didn't say I'd actually do it," she corrected, "just that I'd think about it."

"Well, I've got to be going." Red got up from the chair. "You two can talk about it some more." He pulled his billfold out and walked toward the cashier.

Steven didn't say anything for a few moments; then, giving Kelly a tender look, he said, "I'm glad Red left us alone. I wanted to talk to you. This past weekend meant a lot to me. I hope it meant something to you too." He reached across the table and took her hand.

Slipping it free, Kelly cleared her throat. "As I tried to tell you Sunday morning, I think it's better if we don't. . .get involved with one another."

He only stared at her, saying nothing. She couldn't bring herself to mention seeing the dark-haired girl hug him the day before; she would sound as if she were jealous.

"I'm sorry if I didn't make myself clear."

"I heard what you said," he answered. "You think a man isn't right for you unless he's a Christian. But I think you're wrong about that."

She tried another argument. "Even if I were wrong about that—and I'm not—it still would be very unprofessional on my part to. . ."

"To fall in love?" he finished, his voice tight.

Kelly's eyes flashed to his, then returned to looking in her coffee cup. He couldn't be saying he was falling in love with her; it wasn't possible. Their backgrounds were too dissimilar. Besides, there was the matter of the girl. "If I fall in love," she said, speaking slowly, "it will be with someone who shares my beliefs and goals."

As Steven pushed his chair back it scraped noisily on the wooden floor. He seemed suddenly eager to get away from her. "So, we're going to have that 'ships that pass in the night' routine, are we? Next you'll be telling me we come from different worlds."

She was astonished at the way he had read her mind. But facts were facts, and his sarcasm couldn't change them. "I do hope we can be friends," she continued.

"For the good of the promotion," he snarled. By now he was on his feet. "Well, I'm glad to know where I stand."

"Please don't be angry." Her voice was barely audible.

"Angry? Why should I be angry? You're quite right, of course. We have nothing in common. My fault was in thinking that there was some. . .chemistry between us, something that was more important than whether one went to church or not."

"I'm sorry. I don't want this to—"

"To spoil things? Of course not. We're both professionals and will behave in a professional manner. I won't do anything to spoil your promotion, my dear Miss Marsh. I long ago gave up fruitless grandstand gestures to prove a point!"

This was not going at all the way it should, yet to say anything more would probably only make matters worse. She had to hope he would keep his word and cooperate with her for the balance of the program.

She expected him to stalk off, having made such an impassioned exit speech, but he continued to stand next to the table and stare down at her. She twisted her fingers in her lap.

"So, you're going to take skydiving lessons, are you?" he asked after a long pause.

"No, I'm not. Red tried to persuade me to do it, that is, just take the ground school lessons—I would never jump out of a plane—but I didn't agree to it."

"That figures," he drawled. "You're not the type."

Kelly knew she deserved his rebuke—she'd made a mess of trying to explain her views on their relationship—but something in his tone infuriated her. She raised her chin defiantly and fixed a stern gaze on him. "You don't know me well enough to know what type I am," she said in a smooth, cold voice. "We agreed some time ago, I believe, that I'm willing to learn new things—and since I'm involved in this promotion whether I like it or not, it makes sense for me to learn what preparations skydivers make."

"If you think it's just books and lectures, you're mistaken," he said. "Frankly, I don't think you can take it."

"Can't take it? Yes, I can. I'm no hothouse plant. And Red tells me you don't have to jump for the first few lessons."

"That's true," Steven said. A smile turned up the corners of his generous mouth, and he appeared to know some private joke of which she would be the butt. "But I shouldn't have accused you of not being up to it," he added, his voice heavy with sarcasm. "I'll be there to watch!"

"Don't bother!" Kelly said.

"Oh, but I must," Steven insisted. "You see, I'm the instructor."

Of course he was. He had told her he taught skydiving; how could she have forgotten? She would have backed down at once, but she would have felt too humiliated, so she merely clenched her teeth and tried to keep her face from revealing anything. "As you wish," she said and getting to her feet, snatched up her luncheon check. She was grateful to make a dignified exit, considering the trembling of her legs.

❧

Before Kelly arrived at the field the next day, she read the parachute manual Red had given her. The book called the parachute the safest piece of equipment ever invented and took the next forty pages to tell what could go wrong with it and how to cope with any of those eventualities.

If only she had never allowed Red to believe she would do it—if only Steven had not challenged her to go through with it—she would never have shown up today. But she could not solve problems by running away. She had to continue the promotion, at least for the time being, and must see these people and get along with them. She must keep her word and take the first few lessons. After all, what could happen to her? No one had ever died taking ground school!

There were four young men in the office when Kelly entered, all wearing jumpsuits, standing about talking. At the sight of her, however, the talking stopped and they took in her blond hair tied in a ponytail and the rented yellow jumpsuit she wore. She introduced herself as just another student.

"Have any of you read this manual?" she asked then, holding up the little book she had brought with her. That started a lively discussion about what each of them had already learned, and then Steven entered the room and they sat down.

A small classroom had been created by putting some chairs in a semicircle facing a corner of the office, and there Steven pulled out charts, diagrams, and maps and began his lecture. She was grateful he treated her no differently from the others, neither with deference nor sarcasm, and for the next half hour, Kelly heard a repetition of what she'd read in the manual.

Everything was easier to understand when Steven explained it, and the session was very informal, interrupted from time to time with questions. Then Steven moved to the table displaying a complete, packed parachute and one which was opened but contained no canopy. He explained the metal buckles, fittings, and rip cords, and showed how they worked with the parachute. When that was over, he led them outdoors where, one by one, they practiced stepping out of an airplane.

They used a mockup of an airplane strut and jump step,

and they had to pretend they were exiting from the plane in midair, holding onto the strut and stepping onto the platform, then letting go and jumping into space. When all had done this several times to Steven's satisfaction, they were then asked to lie face down and practice the "frog position," stomachs down, backs arched, arms and legs extended but bent at elbows and knees. They practiced other falling positions too.

Then they returned to the classroom for a lecture about possible malfunctions and emergency procedures. They learned what to do if a parachute inadvertently opened while still in the aircraft or in the doorway; if the main chute didn't open; if both parachutes opened at once, or if the rip cord or static line were dangling; how to jettison a malfunctioning chute; how to land in water, over power lines, in trees, or on buildings.

Kelly wondered what had ever possessed her to agree to take these classes, but she consoled herself by remembering that she was never actually going to jump so could not be exposed to any of the myriad risks Steven discussed so calmly.

Six p.m. arrived quickly. Kelly looked forward to returning to her apartment to a good dinner and an early bedtime. That was before Steven announced that there would be a written test the next day on what they had learned. At midnight she finally closed her weary eyes and then dreamed of parachutes, rip cords, static lines, and altimeters, all jumbled together on top of her, weighing her down. When she awoke she found blanket and sheets wadded up and tangled around her.

Like the four men, Kelly passed the written test; in fact, Steven informed her she had the highest grade and grinned in a way she couldn't understand. She thought he should be unhappy at her success: after all, hadn't he predicted she couldn't do it? She smiled with genuine pleasure while accepting the congratulations of the others. She wanted to pass the test as much because of her feeling of responsibility to her fellow students as her desire to show Steven. She guessed she was caught up in the spirit of it, just as she had always thrown herself wholeheartedly into anything she attempted. In a way she almost regretted that she would never actually need to know any of the procedures she had learned.

She found her opinion of Steven changing as well. He taught brilliantly, bringing each member of the class along step by step, making sure everyone thoroughly understood before going on to the next point. He would have made a fine teacher, she thought. In addition, he further impressed her with his extensive knowledge of the sport and his concern for the safety of its practitioners.

But after the test, she learned he could be a rigid taskmaster as well. Their next assignment was to strap on parachutes and learn how to fall.

"Calf, thigh, buttocks, shoulder," Steven thundered at them, and Kelly muttered the words to herself as she waited in line. How she wished she had been more athletic in school; gymnastics had never been her thing. Now she must throw herself on the ground as if landing after a jump. Of course, the ideal was to touch ground gently on your feet, look as if you were just out for a stroll, but that took lots of practice, and meanwhile you might break a leg until you figured it out.

At her turn, she fell down in a way she hoped was the appropriate somersault type of landing, only to hear the men laugh uproariously at the attempt. Steven said, "Calf and thigh first, Miss Marsh, not buttocks. You don't want to bruise that part of your anatomy, do you?"

Kelly saw nothing funny in it. She did ache from the way she had fallen, but she would not admit it. Once more she got in line and tried again, this time managing to let her legs touch ground first, but she was still not perfect.

"Once more," Steven repeated, and they all moaned and repeated the process.

"And again," he intoned, and by now Kelly surmised her body, protected only marginally by the jumpsuit, must be covered with bruises.

The fact that some of the men also had to repeat the fall did little to improve Kelly's reactions to Steven's sixth repetition of the phrase, "One more time," and she almost agreed with one of her fellow students who muttered under his breath, "If he says, 'one more time,' one more time, I'm gonna strangle him with his own rip cord!"

She actually lost count of the number of times they repeated the maneuver, and just when she thought she could never force her aching body to do it again, he said, in accents reminiscent of Professor Higgins to Eliza Doolittle, "Very good, Miss Marsh, I do believe you've finally got it!"

Kelly managed a weak smile, thankful for the end of that, just as Steven announced, "All right, everybody, now we'll try the same thing from the four-foot platform."

There were no disturbing dreams for Kelly that night; her exhausted body refused to permit them. She soaked for an hour in a hot bath, massaged every muscle she could reach, and then collapsed into bed, vowing she would never go back to that air field. He could threaten her with Chinese water torture and she would not return.

However, the next day, whether propelled by stubbornness, her dedication to seeing everything through to its conclusion, or just a desire to prove to Steven that she could take any punishment he could dish out, she again joined the class, finding some consolation in the fact that the men complained of aching muscles as much as she.

The final classes were to be "easy," Steven advised, leading them to another torture machine which contained harnesses. The students strapped themselves into harnesses and were hoisted up so that they hung about two feet off the ground, and then Steven selected one of various emergency procedures for them each to perform. This gave them the feel of actually being in the air, and having to make maneuvers while dangling from a parachute. There were enough harnesses for only four students at a time, so Steven instructed the men to go first, assuring Kelly that it would be easier once she had seen the others do it.

But when her turn finally came, she decided he had not been altruistic at all, but merely possessed by a devilish desire to see her make a fool of herself all alone. She felt as if she were dangling in the air for a lifetime, going through all the maneuvers, buckling and unbuckling, her hands sometimes refusing to cooperate, pulling on lines and dummy rip cords.

In the last maneuver she had to cut away a malfunctioning parachute and release her emergency. By this time every sore muscle sang its protests, and the men, who had already done the exercise, were resting on the grass, laughing at her discomfort. She resisted the urge to resent their teasing, then concentrated on her task, feet leaden in their heavy boots.

"The parachute is streaming, Miss Marsh," Steven called out. "What do you do?"

"Cut it away?" Kelly shouted back.

"Then do it, Miss Marsh," he ordered.

Kelly went through the correct procedure and then came to the part where she had to pull the release rings to get rid of the main parachute. She yanked at them, but nothing happened. Blaming her feminine hands for being too weak, she yanked again, and this time one of them gave way, leaving her dangling by one strap, hearing a howl of laughter from the men on the ground.

Perspiration stood out on her face, her arms felt as if they were in some giant vise, but her will remained intact. Praying that it would work this time, she reached again for the release ring.

"Don't keep hanging there, my dear lady," Steven shouted. "Grab it and pull it harder."

Kelly's resentment toward Steven mounted, but her discomfort became a more urgent concern. Using both hands on the ring, she pulled as hard as she could. The ring gave way and she fell in a heap on the ground, eyes closed, breathing heavily.

At a sound from above, her eyelids flew open, and she saw Steven bending over her. In a soft whisper she heard him say, "Kelly, that was lovely." Then he added, "But you're dead, you know. You forgot to pull your reserve!"

She clamped her eyes shut again and wished that when she next opened them she'd be on a warm beach in Hawaii with Steven nowhere in sight, but after several minutes in the soft green grass, she struggled to her feet, stalked back to the platform, and climbed into the hated harness once more. In absolute silence—she wondered if the other students were offering their own prayers for her—she went through all the procedures again, pulled the release rings as if they were the only things standing between her and death—and in a way they were—and, as she felt them give way, slammed her hand onto her chest for the emergency rip cord and yanked that as well.

This time as she dropped into the grass, she heard a cheer go up and then everyone clustered around her, hugging her and offering congratulations. Even Steven came up and smiled at her with what appeared to be genuine affection. Her aches and pains were momentarily forgotten as she looked into his eyes. Suddenly, she didn't see the cold-hearted instructor who had put her through such torture. She remembered being in his arms, the touch of his lips on hers. She stopped herself; why had she relived that moment, of all things?

The look on his face gave Kelly the unnerving sensation that he could read her thoughts, that he knew she had undergone a change in her opinion of him during the three-day ordeal. *No,* she told herself adamantly, *I'm not changing my mind about him. He may be a wonderful instructor, and I'm enjoying the fleeting moment of having accomplished something, of having shown him I could do it, but I don't really want to be in his arms again. I'm not falling in love with him. I won't!*

"Well," she said, struggling to keep her voice from betraying the emotions that had just raced through her, "do I pass the course?"

"Yes," he answered, but his eyes seemed to say he was disappointed that she had suddenly hidden the desire for him that had been so blatant in her face only moments before. "You can jump on the static line tomorrow if you like."

"Oh, but I don't like," she answered, pulling off the harness of the emergency pack. "I don't intend to jump at all. I only wanted to take the ground school."

"You haven't learned everything until you jump," he insisted.

"There are some things I don't want to learn."

His gaze raked her face. "That rather contradicts your earlier boast, doesn't it? What else are you afraid of learning, besides skydiving?" Kelly didn't answer. In a voice as sensuous as a caress, he concluded, "I can teach you that too, you know. And I will."

Before Kelly could think of a reply, Steven turned and strode quickly off the field. She realized the other students had already gone, leaving her standing alone in the grass, mixed emotions surging through her.

seven

The long, narrow lake nestled among encircling trees. From her cabin, Kelly could see the lake's sparkling blue tip, looking cool and inviting. Her room was air-conditioned, but she knew that when she stepped out into the brilliant morning sunshine, the heat would hit her like a blast from a furnace, and she dressed in the coolest clothes she'd brought with her the day before, a short cotton skirt, sleeveless cotton blouse, and rope-soled sandals on her bare feet. She pinned her wavy blond hair into a flat bun at the back of her head and added a straw hat with a brim. She added suntan lotion to her arms and legs, then slipped the bottle into her cotton string-tie bag before leaving the cabin.

Kelly had not come to Ogilsby Lake with the others. She drove up the day before, finalized plans for the exhibition, and arranged for cabins for the twelve skydivers. Even Red Johnson had come along for the Independence Day weekend—tomorrow would be July 4th—and everyone had decided to make it a gala holiday.

At first Kelly had been glad to come earlier than the others; this way there would be no question of her riding with Steven Barry in his '57 Thunderbird. Although she continued to feel attracted to him, she vowed to suppress those feelings. But when the caravan of cars had arrived the night before, she had watched as the tall skydiver unwound from his car and then opened the passenger door. The same brunette Kelly had seen with him before stepped out, and Kelly found herself filled with jealousy. She argued that it was no business of hers whom he brought to this event, but somehow the thought failed to comfort her.

The heat had not kept people from attending the exciting event—they were used to summer temperatures in the nineties—and a huge crowd turned out. A grandstand set up next to the airfield with a colorful canvas top of red, white, and blue provided shade, while dozens of flags on tall masts around the field flapped in the summer breeze. A small band, which Kelly had recruited from the local high school, played stirring marches.

Inside the hangar, Kelly checked final details with Steven.

"You've been running around all morning," he said, catching her free hand. "When are you going to relax and enjoy yourself?" He spoke sympathetically, and his cobalt-blue eyes searched hers.

"Soon," she answered, pulling her hand from his warm grip. She put a check mark next to an item on the list fastened to her clipboard. "Your part in the program may be just beginning, but mine is far from over."

"You've done a very good job, by the way."

"Thank you." Kelly enjoyed the sincerity with which he spoke, appreciated what it must have cost him in pride to go from open hostility regarding her participation to admiration. If things were somehow different. . . . But of course they couldn't be.

She consulted her list. "I have you down for the water jump this afternoon, but nothing this morning. Is that right?"

"Yes. I did my quota of acrobatics for the year when I taught the class last week," he joked. "And how are *you* feeling these days? Have you recovered from our three-day exercise?"

"Exercise? Torture test would be more like it. And I'm almost back to normal again, thank you—although I'm sure my arms are two inches longer from hanging in the harness!"

"If they are, it's very becoming," he said, moving closer to her. "What about lunch?"

"There will be a break for lunch, of course. People may picnic on the lawn between the field and the lake. Although we have food vendors, most visitors have probably brought their own lunches. I've arranged for some beach umbrellas to be set up, as well as the redwood tables and benches among the trees, so people can have a place to eat and a little shade from the sun."

"Whoa," Steven said. "I wasn't asking about your arrangements. I wanted to have lunch with you."

Considering how boldly she had rejected him a week ago, and his anger at that time, Kelly was surprised at his good humor today. For some reason he seemed ready to resume his attempt at what he had called "more than friendship." But why? Had the ground school lessons that she'd taken given him a different impression of her? Or did he still think she might fall in love with him? But, more importantly, what about the girl he brought with him? She wanted to ask if he planned to lunch with her, but instead she murmured, "I thought you never eat before a jump?"

"I don't. But you do. Can't I watch?" He grinned.

Kelly had to laugh in spite of the conflicting emotions he continued to stir in her. "That doesn't sound like much fun."

"Let me be the judge of that."

Biting her lip for a moment, Kelly threw caution to the wind. "What about the young lady you brought here last night? Won't she object to your spending your free time with me?"

"Young lady?" Steven repeated, his look thoughtful. "Oh,

you mean Hayley."

"You haven't introduced us."

"That's because she's never where she's supposed to be," he said irritably. "Besides, everyone knows Hayley—I've been dragging her around to jumps since she was six. She's my little cousin."

Kelly felt her heart turn over. His cousin; that explained everything. She tried to hide her sigh of relief, but Steven noted her reaction. A broader smile than usual spread across his face.

"Were you jealous of her?"

"Of course not."

"Then have lunch with me."

"All right," she agreed, "but I must go now. It's starting time." She fled before he could see the red flush creep up her face.

Like one of the paying customers, Kelly sat in the grandstand to watch the events, forcing herself to concentrate on them instead of Steven. First came aerial acrobatics, with the jumpers performing dives, loops, turns, and backloops in sequence. Watching the smoke flares attached to the jumpers' boots enabled her to keep track of them despite their altitude. Then there were formation jumps, four men making a diamond or other shape in the sky; and then three women came down together, holding a giant American flag.

Finally a "star"—actually a circle of skydivers—took shape. Excitement ran high as the divers leapt from the aircraft and linked up with their hands. Although Kelly had been told there were often twenty- and thirty-diver stars, and that the record stood at more than seventy, she was as thrilled as anyone else there. The audience applauded and whistled loudly when the twelve-pointed "star" was completed. Then the jumpers broke from one another, and opened their parachutes.

With lunchtime came a problem she had to solve, leaving no chance to look for Steven, and the afternoon event was ready before she had finished. She saw Steven standing on the field, checking out the equipment on each of the men: first their two parachutes, then the flotation device for the water landing, and finally a waterproof bag for their instruments.

"You stood me up," he accused when she approached, although his voice showed no sign of resentment.

"I'm sorry. I had to settle a mix-up about the security guards. It's all right now."

"Speaking of guards," he said, not looking up from his task, "you did arrange for people with life-saving experience to be in the boats, didn't you?" His forehead wrinkled into a frown.

"Of course," Kelly said matter-of-factly, and she hoped that the young men she had hired were indeed as good as they were supposed to be. All of the skydivers could swim, she'd been told, and all had made water jumps before, but it was reassuring to know that someone would be available in each boat to help if he was needed.

Steven handed a waterproof bag to one of the men and watched him attach it to his chest pack. "Water will ruin an altimeter," he explained to Kelly, "although not all of the men are taking one along on this jump."

"Why not? I thought an altimeter was always necessary."

"Not always. It's true that there's less depth perception over water than over land, and jumpers have been known to be injured by thinking they were only a few feet above the water when actually they were forty or fifty feet above. But the boats will give them a point of reference today. Besides, the current rules say they don't let go of the harness until their feet touch the water."

"My schedule says only six of them go up at a time. Is that right?"

He nodded. "We need a jumper in each boat. Then we'll take turns." He looked at her and winked. "Want to come along and jump with us?"

"Not on your life!" she said, laughing. "But I might watch you from one of the rowboats."

"Great." He gave her hand a squeeze and headed for the plane.

Kelly ran the entire distance from field to lake and was just in time to see the six small rowboats, two men in each, push off from the sandy beach to get into position to pick up the skydivers as they landed in the water. She shouted to Gary Nelson, who was wading next to one of the boats, "Gary, may I go with you?"

"Sure," he said. "Come aboard."

Kelly pulled off her shoes, leaving them in the sand, and waded into the cool clear water, feeling it splash up on her legs. She scrambled aboard, and the other young man, a teenager wearing only swim trunks and a tan, helped her to the middle seat. Water swishing softly against the sides of the boat, they rowed to the middle of the lake and, with the other five boats, formed a large circle.

Then Pete, the lifeguard, put on swim fins and slipped a swim mask onto his head, where it rested in his tightly curled, sun-bleached hair. Thus prepared, they watched the jumpers leave the aircraft one at a time, free-fall for several seconds, then open their parachutes and maneuver them toward the target in the center, a rubber life raft with a bull's-eye painted on cloth.

One by one they landed near the target, and as soon as they did, the boat which had been assigned to that jumper went out and picked him up. Kelly's boat picked up the last jumper of that group, and she watched in fascination as they gathered in the parachute and then dragged it ashore. Gary left to take his turn in the air, and the man they had brought back to shore peeled off his jumpsuit, shoes, and helmet, revealing his swim trunks underneath, and got into the rowboat again, ready to be the experienced skydiver required by regulation to be in the boat.

Again they were to pick up the last jumper, and Kelly realized with pleasure that it would be Steven. He usually came last in any of the exhibitions, being jumpmaster, but he was also the best. Watching him leave the aircraft, Kelly felt a surge of pride, as if she were somehow responsible for his superior performance. His jumpsuit whiter than chalk in the sky, he spread his arms and legs for his stable free fall.

She looked up, unheeding of the ache in her neck from constant sky-watching, and thrilled as his chute opened and the colorful canopy snapped him upward for a few feet before it began its descent to the water. She thought she could almost see him begin to unfasten the harness buckles that held him in the parachute and get ready to release it so that he would not be dragged down with the fabric when it became heavy and waterlogged.

As usual, he landed right on target, his feet touching lightly onto the bull's-eye on the raft. Then he let go of the handles on the chute and it drifted above him momentarily and finally settled on the surface of the water only inches away.

Pete rowed to the spot, and Kelly watched Steven slip off the raft into the water, reaching for the chute before it had time to sink. The sight of him, immersed to his chin, brought a rush of emotion. She stood up in the boat, leaning forward to help him pull in the soggy parachute.

"Sit down," Pete said to her. "We can handle it."

She sat down obediently, but never took her eyes from Steven's head as he tugged at his equipment in the water. Then, to her horror, she saw him slip beneath the surface.

"Steven!" She thought she screamed, but his name came out only a whisper. Before anyone saw her, she dove head first into the lake and under the enormous parachute. Eyes open, she saw Steven untangling the lines of the chute which had somehow become caught in the cable holding the life raft to its anchor. Her splash had alerted him and he watched her descend, looking surprised.

Suddenly she realized what a stupid thing she had done. She was underwater, hair streaming, skirt swirling about her waist. She had tried to help a man who needed no help, and she knew she looked foolish and unnecessary. But before she could turn about and swim away, she became a prisoner of the parachute. It continued to descend and she was sucked underneath. She fought its clinging folds, trying to get down and around it, but she was trapped. Panic rose. She couldn't hold her breath much longer.

A strong arm grasped her around the neck and shoulders and pulled her forcefully in the other direction. She felt herself dragged down and thought, *We're drowning,* but just as suddenly, the water became lighter in color, sparkling with sunlight. She discovered Steven had pulled her away from the chute and they were surfacing.

She broke water with a sputter and drinking heavily of the fresh air, stared at her rescuer. He glared at her, disgust written on his features. "Don't ever do such a dumb thing again. You could have drowned."

"I was only—"

"You were only in over your head again, this time literally." His words were clear, but his voice sounded tense. He turned and pushed her toward the rowboat, which by now had come toward them, and boosting her up, shoved her into the waiting arms of the two young men in the boat.

She huddled on the wooden seat, hugging her arms around her drenched body, and wished she had stayed in the water and drowned. Anything would be better than this humiliation.

"Gee, Miss Marsh," Pete said, throwing his discarded shirt over her shoulders. "I'm awfully sorry. I should have been watching. I didn't realize I tipped the boat so far that you fell overboard. But you shouldn't have been standing, you know."

"But you didn't," she started to explain, then stopped. Pete had gone back to pulling the parachute to the side of the boat, and he was no longer listening to her. Anyway, let them think it was an accident. That was better than the truth.

Steven clambered aboard and grabbed an oar, helping Pete row the craft back to the beach. As soon as it scraped the sand, Kelly leaped out and ran. Her day spoiled, she would go back to her cabin and never come out.

Inside, she threw herself down on her bed and wept tears of frustration. How could she have been so stupid? Why had she dived into the water, as if Steven were a child who needed to be rescued? Why had she suddenly felt so protective toward him? The feelings he stirred within her were too strong to be denied anymore. That Steven Barry had become the object of her every waking thought was more than disturbing; it constituted a distinct problem, one she would have to overcome. Why did she care for a man who was so obviously unsuitable for her?

As she lay on the bed, tears finally drying on her face,

the unpleasant truth came. She had been judging the man, thinking he was unworthy of her! Her heart pounded in her ears, as the full impact of her behavior struck. She had put herself on a pedestal and believed that Steven, a man who made his living at something she could not approve, was beneath her.

And not only Steven. All her adult life she had been judging men and finding them lacking. They were too pushy, too arrogant, too chauvinistic. When they reacted to her good looks, she dubbed them shallow and sensuous, only interested in one thing. No wonder she never formed a close relationship with a man; she immediately found fault with all of them. Unless they looked as she thought they should, spoke the proper language with the correct inflection, did the things she approved of, she had written them off. No human being could possibly live up to the unrealistic standards she set. To want a man who was a Christian was one thing, but she had given no one a chance to understand why a relationship with Christ was important; she had turned men away before they could get close enough to even see that Christ truly lived within her. She turned her face against the pillow, praying for forgiveness and humility.

❧

Hours later, hunger gnawed at her and she turned with a start; she had fallen asleep on the bed. Darkness had settled over the lake, and she realized that what had awakened her, besides an interior rumbling, was the sound of fireworks. Reluctantly, she decided she had to go to the beach and join the others. Even if she were not in need of the picnic supper she had arranged—and she really was, since she'd missed lunch—she would be expected to show up, if only for a few minutes.

After changing clothes, she smoothed her hair and slipped from the cabin, slowly walking across the dirt road and over grassy slopes toward the beach. She approached the crowd there with some trepidation, but everyone greeted her warmly, and no one seemed to know, or remember, the boat incident. The skydivers had made two fires of driftwood, and Kelly joined one, roasting hot dogs and passing around huge paper containers of potato salad, bean salad, and cole slaw. The buns were soft and warm and the relish tasty; normally Kelly didn't care for hot dogs, but she had to admit they were delicious tonight.

Other fires, marking other picnics, glowed on the beach, as many of the townspeople had stayed to watch the fireworks arranged by Kelly and the local Kiwanis Club. After the brilliant display concluded, and the sky deepened from blue to black, the picnickers drifted back to their homes, leaving only the skydivers, who would not be going back to town for another day.

Gary Nelson had brought his guitar, and as he played folk songs, Kelly joined in singing the familiar words, glad now she had come. Then someone shouted, "You know what?" He answered his own question with, "It's too hot!"

"Let's go swimming," someone else suggested, and soon they rushed to their cabins to change into swimsuits and plunge into the water. Kelly went back to her cabin and changed too.

The water was almost as warm as the surrounding air, but there was something mystical about swimming in the dark. The others laughed and shouted, playing games in the water, and some of the men and their girlfriends paired off, sitting on the sandy bottom with water up to their chins, hugging and kissing, whispering endearments.

Kelly felt superfluous and swam out to the raft anchored

not far away. Pulling herself up, she rested on its slippery wooden surface for a few moments, then retied the ribbon around her hair and took a few deep breaths before getting ready to drop into the water and swim back to the beach.

Suddenly she felt a touch on her foot and gasped. The water broke in front of her and a head bobbed to the surface. Steven.

"You startled me," she said. "I didn't see you swim up."

"I came the last twenty yards under water." Drops ran from his chiseled features, dripped from his mat of black hair, and glistened on his exposed muscular shoulders. Kelly felt strange. The excitement she found in his company remained, but added to it was her new awareness of his true self, a person she could admire and respect, whether he ever shared her beliefs or not.

He pulled himself effortlessly onto the raft and sat next to her. Silence enveloped them, and she tried to think of something to say. Her heart seemed ready to burst with love for all her fellow human beings, Steven included, but the lesson she had just learned seemed too precious to share, at least for now.

"I came to apologize for my rude behavior this afternoon," he said. "It was unforgivable, since you were obviously trying to save my life. Later, I felt—" He shook his head and turned toward her. When he spoke again, his voice was so soft she could barely hear him. "Thank you, Kelly."

Kelly had tried to forget the episode, but his words reminded her, and her throat constricted.

"The truth is," he continued, his voice still soft, "you scared me so much that I shouted at you without thinking. I know you don't feel the same toward me as I do toward you, but that was no excuse for me to take my hurt feelings out on you."

"Steven, it's I who should apologize. I did a very foolish thing and endangered your life as well as my own. Not only that, I've acted vain and proud toward you. Please forgive me."

Steven's expression changed; dejection turned to surprise, then gave way to joy as he captured her hand and held it to his lips. "There's nothing to forgive. I've deserved every unkind thought and word. I acted like a male chauvinist, tried to prove you couldn't do your job, and finally—"

"No, no," she interrupted. "It was all my fault. I disliked you from the first, without ever getting to know you. That was wrong." She pulled her hand away and drew up her knees, hugging them to her with both arms, looking at the inky blackness of the water instead of his penetrating gaze. "I had this stupid idea that people should behave in. . .certain ways. . . ."

"Like not jumping out of airplanes for a living?"

"Something like that. But now I realize what a grave mistake it is to label people, to believe that some are more worthy than others."

"Are you saying what I think you're saying?" he asked. "You know I care about you more than any other woman I've ever met. Is it possible that it's reciprocated, just a little?"

Kelly breathed deeply, laboriously, as if she had swum miles instead of a short distance. She knew she must be honest and speak the truth.

"I've changed my mind about you, yes. But you must understand that I'm not in a position to talk about anything more than that. I still believe that Christians should not become involved—romantically, that is—with non-Christians. But—uh, yes, I do like you very much."

After a pause, he said, "I guess I'll have to be content

with that for the moment. I've been such an idiot, provoking you, testing you. But I know now I was just trying to deny the overwhelming feelings I had for you. You see, you're so totally different from other women I've met." He paused again and then chuckled. "You're that churchgoing lady with the high ideals."

"But you come from a churchgoing family yourself. At least I saw your father at my church last week."

"My mother provided all the religion in our family. She sent me to Sunday school, but it didn't take. When she died, I . . ." In spite of their new openness, Steven seemed reluctant to continue. Kelly suspected memories he had long ago suppressed were surging in on him, making him uncomfortable.

"It's all right," she said, placing a hand on his arm. "You don't have to talk about it if you don't want to. I think it's getting cooler—shall we swim back to the beach?"

Steven shook off his somber mood. "All right," he said, his voice lighter again. "Let's race. I'll give you a head start."

Kelly slipped from his touch and jumped over the side of the raft. Then she was swimming, stroking effortlessly on the gentle ripples of the water. She was glad they were friends now, but she wondered if she'd done the right thing by admitting some of what she felt for him.

How complicated life had become.

eight

Her bed sheets a wrinkled mass on her bed, the flowered spread thrown carelessly to the floor, Kelly woke from a restless night, reliving the events of the weekend.

Before she drove home from the lake, she and Steven spent the day together, swimming, boating, walking in the woods—and especially talking.

"When you were a little girl," he asked, as they hiked around the southern end of the lake, "did you wear your hair in a ponytail with a ribbon in it?"

"Two ponytails," Kelly corrected, "one on each side. And the ribbons always came undone."

"Your ribbons came undone?" he scoffed, and he turned on the narrow path to give her a look of disbelief. "Other children's ribbons, perhaps, but not yours. I can't imagine you as anything less than Miss Perfect, right to the tips of your ponytails."

"I was a normal child," she insisted. She picked up a loose twig from the ground and threw it playfully at him. "It was only later that I became perfect."

His laugh sounded through the clear air. Then he asked, "When did you begin to read to the blind?"

"It was during high school. My church youth group provided lots of worthwhile services for others, including reading to the people at the retirement home. Then the pastor of my church suggested I might read for the blind, because he thought I had a pleasant voice and good articulation."

"A very pleasant voice," Steven agreed.

"I suppose there's a little of the actress in all young girls, and I loved putting feeling into what I read."

"What kinds of books did you read?"

"Every kind, almost. Best-sellers sometimes. But then a college student needed to have his textbooks put on tape so he could keep up with his classes, and I did that for two years."

"That lilt in your voice tells me you enjoyed it. Was this college student charming? Did you fall in love with him?"

Kelly felt her heart beat stronger. Could Steven be jealous of a blind boy? If so, it showed that he realized that inner qualities, and not mere physical prowess, made people lovable. "No, I didn't fall in love with him."

Steven stopped and put his arms on her shoulders, kissing the tip of her nose. "I'm glad you were saving yourself for me. I'm not blind, but I need you too."

She looked up at him quizzically. "You need me? What can *I* do for *you*?"

After a pause, he pushed her gently away. "Oh, I'll think of something." He laughed and resumed walking.

"And what did you do in high school?" Kelly asked.

"All the usual things, baseball in the spring, football in the fall, basketball in the winter. . ."

"And in the summer?"

"Worked in one of my father's companies. Every year it was a different one, some of them quite far away. He wanted me to learn about them all."

"It sounds like a very good idea."

"I suppose. That way, when I took over as president. . ." He cleared his throat loudly before he continued, ". . .I wouldn't be resented because of being the boss's son."

"How perceptive of your father."

"A genius, no doubt about it," Steven answered, but his

voice had taken on a hard edge.

"Your father—" Kelly began.

Steven interrupted her. "I don't want to talk about my father. Let's change the subject. I'd rather talk about you. Your life is far more interesting than mine."

"More interesting?" Kelly laughed. "All I did was go to school and to church and read for the blind."

"But you found it interesting, and that's what counts."

"And you didn't think *your* life was—every summer in a different plant, learning new and different things?"

"I resented it. First of all, you have to remember I was in a private school. I wasn't at home with my parents during the school term. So when summer came, I wanted to be there, and he wouldn't let me."

"Did you tell him how you felt about it?"

Again a long pause. "No, I couldn't tell him. He never seemed to understand me. He was so much older."

"Could you tell your mother and ask her. . . ?"

"My mother died when I was sixteen. I was away at school and I didn't even know she was sick until it was too late. I received a telephone call in the middle of the night, and by the time I arrived home, it was all over. I never got to say good-bye to her." His last words were barely audible, and his pace had accelerated so that he was taking huge strides down the path. Kelly was almost running to keep up with him.

"Steven, please slow down. Steven, I'm so sorry."

"Why should you be sorry?" He stopped and turned to her, his features twisted into a mask of hatred. "It wasn't your fault."

"It was no one's fault." She stared into his eyes. "You blame him, don't you?" she asked with sudden realization. "You blame your father."

"I'm an adult now. I don't blame him anymore."

"I think you still do."

"I said I don't want to talk about it." Again he turned and marched off down the path, and Kelly knew it was pointless to attempt to continue the discussion. When they returned to the cabin, he suggested a swim, and later in the day he told about his first airplane ride and his first parachute jump, and once again their conversation was easy and comfortable. Feeling he would eventually come to trust her, she did not press him for other memories he was so reluctant to dredge from his past.

In spite of their growing closeness and Kelly's new attempt to be open-minded, some doubts still remained in her mind. She and Steven were becoming serious about each other; something in each of them had a magnetic pull to the other. She cared for him—but not enough to commit her life to him when she knew he did not believe in Christ the way she did.

&

Now she gave up trying to sleep and ran the water for a long soak in the tub. Sitting there, she made an effort to switch her thoughts to her job; another exhibition faced her. Soon the six events would be over, and what would happen to her relationship with Steven then?

She remembered how she had argued to be relieved of this assignment, and how she had longed to plan the opera benefit instead. Three weeks had passed since she spoke to Mr. Trask about that. Perhaps he had good news for her and hadn't been able to reach her. She'd have to telephone him.

But when she called the next day before leaving for work, she was informed he was away for a few days and would return her call later.

Kelly drove to her office and plunged into the mail that had accumulated. Her boss appeared at her doorway. "I haven't seen you for a week," Lyle said. "I've missed you."

Kelly smiled briefly, then returned her gaze to her desk. "This promotion is much more complicated than I ever imagined. You wouldn't believe the amount of paperwork involved."

Lyle seemed on the verge of coming into her office, but then changed his mind, fingering the doorknob as if nervous about something. "Let's have lunch?" he asked. "There are a few things I'd like to talk to you about."

Kelly hesitated, and then, realizing his request was a business command and not a social engagement, she acquiesced.

She had accomplished much by the time they went to the French restaurant, and since she loved the delicate flavors of French cooking, she enjoyed the meal thoroughly. As they finished with creme caramel for dessert, Lyle finally brought the conversation around to business.

"I should be angry with you," he began.

"Why?" Kelly asked, her eyes widening.

"Because you went over my head. That just isn't done, you know." His friendly tone belied his somber words.

"I don't understand," she said.

"You went to see Christopher Trask, to try to get his support for the opera promotion."

Kelly felt her pulse speed up and her face grow warm. She had forgotten about that, hadn't realized Mr. Trask might contact her boss instead of her. What a fool she'd been not to discuss it with Lyle in advance. Now what would happen? Would he retract his promise to let her do the opera promotion?

"I'm sorry," she said, pushing her half-eaten dessert away

and looking down into the snowy white napkin in her lap. "I shouldn't have done that. I'm afraid I acted without thinking."

"Impulsive gestures frequently get people into trouble," he said, "although I can understand why you did it."

She looked up at him again. "You can?"

"Yes. I haven't known you very long, but I think I've learned quite a bit about your character already. You plunge into whatever you're doing with such enthusiasm and energy—trying always to do the best—you sometimes get carried away."

"Yes, I guess I do, but—"

"I knew you wanted the opera benefit more than anything else. I should have anticipated, I suppose, that after I made that promise, you might try something like this, just to get out of the skydiving events."

"Oh, it wasn't that!" Kelly protested, although she knew that certainly had been her original purpose. Then, flustered at having told a lie, she squirmed, twisting the napkin around her fingers, and continued, "I mean, it wasn't just that. Yes, I did want to get out of the sports promotion, because as I told you, I simply didn't feel qualified to do it, and I'd wanted the other for so very long."

"But you're doing a splendid job, just as I knew you would."

"Thank you, but at the time. . .well. . ." She stopped, realizing she certainly couldn't go much further down this line of explanation. She couldn't tell Lyle what had transpired between her and Steven. She had never discussed her love life with others. Besides, she really did want to do the opera promotion, even though it would suit her purposes better now if it were to come *after* the skydiving exhibitions were over. Somehow she couldn't find words to explain her change of heart to Lyle, especially in view of her visit to Mr. Trask.

"I'm trying to do a good job of the skydiving promotion," she finished lamely.

"I know you are," Lyle acknowledged, "and believe me, I'm not angry about what you did. In a way I approve your obvious enthusiasm and the fact that you showed resourcefulness in visiting the man to organize things. After I got over my initial embarrassment when Mr. Trask telephoned and I had to admit I had no idea you'd been to see him, I came to the realization that you are a person, like me, who believes first and foremost in getting things done."

The emphasis when he said, "like me," caused Kelly to look into his eyes and see admiration. She looked away.

He paused before continuing. "Well, I didn't mean to scold you. I hope you don't think that."

"No, no, I understand."

"I'm very pleased with your work. You and I are a great team, Kelly. I felt we would be right from the start, and you confirm my opinion every day. I just wish I could see you more often. Would you have dinner with me tomorrow night?"

Kelly hadn't expected this and was startled. She had noticed his strong attraction to her right from the beginning, and although she had turned down his invitation for dinner after the Park Side promotion, she hadn't expected him to give up entirely. But so much had happened since then, she had really forgotten Lyle. Now, she must explain about Steven or else hide her feelings. But what could she tell him? To admit she might be falling in love with Steven would seem very unprofessional to him. He might pull her off the assignment for that reason alone. At the same time, she could hardly accept his dinner invitation.

Had this happened before she met Steven, she might have been delighted to accept. Men of his type normally attracted her, more so than Steven's. He was established in business, talented, and even good-looking, although in a much different way from Steven. And if, as he hinted, they had much in common regarding their goals, then it would have made sense for her to get to know him better. But now it was clearly impossible.

"I'm afraid not," she said. "Tomorrow I have to drive to Fairmount about the exhibition there and probably won't get back until the next day. Then there's this week's promotion. . ."

"Perhaps next week?"

"Next week I'll be in Fairmount."

"Then I suppose it will have to be the week after that."

Kelly laughed. "I do seem to be inaccessible, but it's all in the line of business."

The waiter came, and Lyle laid his credit card on the tray with the bill. "Then I guess I can't complain about it. But let's make it definite after the promotion, shall we?" He pulled out a pocket calendar and marked in it with his pen.

Kelly knew she should explain why she didn't want to have dinner with him, but somehow she couldn't. Normally she didn't put off doing unpleasant but necessary things, but this was her boss. She needed diplomacy, a trait she didn't think she had just now. And besides, how could she explain that she didn't want to go out with Lyle because she was falling in love with a man to whom she could never commit herself? How could he understand when she didn't even understand herself?

❧

For the balance of the week, all her efforts were expended

on planning the next two jumps. This week's exhibit would be close by—in Parkfield—a night jump into a circle of lights.

Steven appeared on the field wearing a silver jumpsuit. She guessed he'd chosen it because it would sparkle in the night sky when the lights shone on it. She pulled the red scarf from her neck and put it around his.

"What's this for?" he asked, as she tied it in place.

"Your jumpsuit looks like armor, and when the knights went into battle, they always wore a scarf, didn't they?"

"It was given by the ladies who waited for them to return safely. Are you staking your claim on me?"

Kelly wondered if she was committing herself more thoroughly than she had a right to at this time, considering the turmoil in her heart over their differences. "We'll talk about that later," she said, and then Red Johnson approached so she didn't have to explain.

"Reminds me of the old days," Red told them, rubbing his chin thoughtfully and smiling. "I used to love night jumps."

"Well, come on," Steven urged. "Come with me."

"No, no," he protested. "I'm too old to jump any more. Anyway, you're teasing me. It's your show. You're the star!"

Steven tilted his head back and his laugh carried across the park. "I'm not a star," he denied. "I'm just a guinea pig. They push me around here and there, doing stunts so someone can make some money for charity."

"But people look up to you, like you're special," Red continued. "Don't tell me—I know all about it. I used to love that feeling myself. Hey, doesn't everyone like to be the center of attention?"

Steven's eyes told Kelly a different story. He smiled no

smile, laughed no laugh now. But if he hadn't gone into skydiving for the adulation of the crowd, then why had he done it? It was one of the subjects he would never discuss.

Her thoughts were interrupted by an official from the park, and for the next hour she took care of final details and double-checked that everyone was certain about his tasks. She had no qualms about Steven performing perfectly, so she left him and turned her attention to the men with the lights.

The buffet party held before the jump raised funds for the charity. People were dressed in party clothes, mingling in the balmy summer air of evening, strolling on the lawn, leaving their empty punch glasses everywhere except the receptacles provided.

Then at last, with the sky dark, Steven's plane took off from the nearby air strip, and the spectators found their vantage points to watch the jump. The lights of the little pavilion flickered out, leaving only the circle of lights made by strategically parked cars.

Her work done, Kelly watched as Steven, a mere dot in the sky, left the plane and began his descent. Battery-powered lights, about the size of flashlights, were fastened to his wrists and ankles, so that as he fell to earth, she spotted him against the darkened heavens. Then his parachute opened and a spotlight flooded on, illuminating the interior of it, like a giant cradle of light. Brighter and brighter he became, his silver jumpsuit shimmering like a shiny coin, and then he landed in the exact center of the circle of beams from the cars.

A crowd of people rushed forward, and Kelly watched from a distance as they crowded around him, the young girls touching his jumpsuit, shoving autograph books at him. He smiled at everyone and seemed to enjoy this part too, in spite of the look she had seen on his face earlier. Or was he just playing a part? She sighed. At times, under her gentle probing, she'd learned a little more about his childhood, but except for skydiving, the years between sixteen and the present were largely a mystery. She felt left out of large parts of his life, and she didn't know how to penetrate without making him angry.

&

When Steven's Thunderbird stopped in front of her office and he stepped out onto the curb, Kelly was as nervous as a little girl meeting her kindergarten teacher for the first time. In the three days since she'd seen him, she had come to a decision. She'd use the three-hour drive to Fairmount to straighten things out with him. He could not get away or avoid her, and she'd insist he let her in on the past that lay buried somewhere within him. She was certain she could help him overcome the unhappiness that clouded it. He seemed to care very much for her; on every subject but himself, he was open and honest. Yet how could their relationship grow when he so skillfully avoided discussing what troubled him? How could she even hope he would let Christ into his life when he so stubbornly refused to let her into parts of it?

"Good morning." She greeted him warmly, and he kissed her briefly before she entered the car. As he steered the vehicle away from the curb and into the traffic, he said, "Red Johnson is coming with us. We're picking him up at his apartment."

So they were not to be alone on the long drive after all. Kelly almost sighed aloud. Well, she would have to find some other time during the long weekend. That ought not to be too difficult. Some of her strain evaporated, and she realized she had been dreading the confrontation, however much she understood its necessity.

Within minutes they had picked up Red, and the three headed out of town. Seated close to Steven, feeling the warmth of his right arm against her shoulder, Kelly enjoyed the drive, although she barely spoke at all for the first hour. Steven and Red kept up a steady stream of conversation, commenting on flying, jumping, parachutes and other equipment, and on old times. She so loved hearing about the escapades they had in the past, that she almost forgot her anxiety and relaxed.

Steven apologized for their having talked over her head for many miles, and then the three discussed more common topics until they were finally high in the Los Padres National Forest, beyond which lay their destination.

The road wound slowly up the mountains, where trees were tall and close together. Gradually their conversation slowed until it ceased altogether, and gradually too a realization came to Kelly that something was not quite right. An acrid odor hung in the air, and she realized the sky above was no longer blue, but gray.

Just as she started to ask about it, Steven snapped on the car radio, saying, "I think there's a fire somewhere."

After fiddling with the dial for some seconds, he finally found a news station, and amidst crackling of static, they heard the announcer say that the dry hot summer had resulted in a forest fire in the Los Padres Forest. Soon they approached a sign on the highway which read, "Fire Danger High," and a little farther, at a fork in the road, a forest ranger could be seen setting up a road block. They stopped in front of him.

"Take this road to the left," the ranger commanded.

"Where's the fire?" Steven asked.

"About five miles from here. Too close for safety. You'll

have to get down this way." Again he waved them toward the other road.

"Which way is the ranger station?" Steven asked then. "Are there any smoke jumpers there? I'm a parachutist."

The ranger came closer to the car. "If you want to volunteer, come with me. I'm going near there now on my way to set up another barricade."

Steven pulled on the emergency brake, then he quickly stepped out and went around to the trunk.

"What are you doing?" Kelly's heart pounded as she suddenly realized he intended to leave them and go off with the ranger.

"I'm going to volunteer," he responded through tight lips, lifting out parachutes and suitcases.

"What does that mean?"

"Smoke jumping," Red answered for Steven. "We've all done it. You jump into the area and help fight the fire."

"But you're not firemen," Kelly protested. "You're skydivers. I don't understand."

Red explained patiently. "Lots of sport parachutists also become smoke jumpers. They jump into a forest fire area where other ways might be impossible. They can help contain the fire or even put it out."

By now Steven had retrieved the gear he wanted and hauled it to the ranger's car at the side of the road. Kelly ran to him. "What about the promotion?" she asked, her face taut.

"Postpone it," he said quickly, not turning to look at her.

"Postpone it? Do you realize how much work went into this? Do you understand the plans that will have to be changed, the schedules, the people that will be inconvenienced?"

Steven turned and stared down at her with an intense

look. "No," he said in a low voice. "I don't know about inconvenience. People live here. Their lives are in danger. That's all I care about right now. If I can help stop the fire from spreading, that's my responsibility, not some ridiculous promotion!"

"Ridiculous?" Kelly echoed. "You didn't think it so ridiculous when you signed a contract for money to do it!"

"Don't you understand?" he almost shouted. "This is more important! I'm an experienced smoke jumper. I have to go."

Kelly felt anger, frustration, and fear all at once. The smell of smoke had become heavier in just the few minutes they remained there, and the sky seemed darker. She even felt warmer, as if the fire already touched her bare arms.

Then she thought about Steven jumping into it with his parachute. Would the chute catch fire? Would the smoke overcome him? If skydiving itself was dangerous, then what about smoke jumping? It sounded like a suicide mission.

Her heart beating faster, Kelly clung to Steven's arm. "They didn't call you to come," she pleaded, tears suddenly stinging her eyes. "You don't have to do this!"

Steven stowed his belongings in the ranger's car, then turned once more to Kelly, who was standing in the road, feet apart, fists clenched at her sides, eyes swimming with tears, yet with a stubborn tilt to her chin. His face softened.

"Don't be afraid for me. I'll be all right. I'm sorry about your promotion—really I am—but you just have to understand." Then, before she could reply, he swept her into his arms and gave her a hard, passionate kiss that left her breathless. "Say your funny little prayers for me, won't you?"

"You know I will." Kelly accepted the pointlessness of

continuing to argue with him. He was a stubborn man and had made up his mind.

Then he turned her about by her shoulders and pointed her toward the Thunderbird. "Take my car down," he said. "I'll be here for two or three days probably."

"But how—what?" she protested, as she stumbled toward the car with blurred vision.

"Don't worry," he said again. "I'll get someone to bring me back when we're through. Red," he added, "take care of her." Then he jumped into the other vehicle and it sped off.

Kelly stood helplessly in the road, watching the departing car, upset over Steven's decision to leave her, worried for his safety, and feeling frustrated and impotent. It wasn't fair!

She wanted to stand still and cry, but the moment passed quickly. No longer a child throwing a temper tantrum, she must behave like a grown woman, and a practical one at that. She knew she must accept the situation and make the best of it.

Red, who had been silent during the last few minutes, spoke quietly to her. "Do you want me to drive?"

"No," she said firmly, "I'll do it." She climbed in behind the wheel, glad to have something physical to do.

Grim-faced, biting her lip to keep back the tears, she sped off on the left-hand road, and they descended the mountain. After a quarter of an hour, the strain gradually began to leave her, and Red, sensing her relaxation, began to talk.

"Don't worry," he said. "It's not all that dangerous." In a slow, soft voice he related to her how smoke jumpers worked; they jumped into the area with protective covering, carrying axes and shovels, and blocked the progress of the fire.

Kelly listened, her mind only half on his words, the other part beginning to wonder how she would postpone the promotion, rearrange so many plans.

Red told her about his own experiences smoke jumping, about the time he had to dig a trench for himself and cover it with earth when he was trapped in the path of an approaching fire. "And see," he added, "I'm still alive!"

"Oh, Red, you are a good friend. Thank you for telling me. I can't help being a little afraid, though."

"Oh, he'll come back okay," Red assured her. "He's very resourceful. Besides he has you to come back to."

Kelly whirled her head around to him and saw the smug, "I know your secret" look on his face. After what he had seen, he could easily imagine she and Steven were in love. "Oh, Red, I didn't mean for things to get this serious, and now I feel so—so trapped."

"Sure," he said. "I understand."

"I never wanted to fall in love with Steven. I'm not even sure he feels the same way toward me."

"I've known Steven a long time. I'd say he's in love with you all right."

"At first," she insisted, "we quarreled all the time. Perhaps he still thinks me young, stupid, and incompetent."

"No," Red contradicted. "It seems to me he knows how good you are at your job. Even so, I'm sure it hasn't been easy for him. At first, he just saw you as a pretty young lady. Pretty ladies have been hanging around him for years."

"But I don't know what to do about him. I think I'm in love with him, but most of the time I don't want to be."

"He isn't the easiest man in the world to love—at least not at first—but give him time."

"I'm trying to understand him, but sometimes he makes

it so difficult, especially when he refuses to discuss the past. There are things he simply won't talk about." Her voice rose in pitch, and she realized she sounded like a sulky child. She didn't really want to be petty.

"Oh, well," Red answered, a shrug in his voice, "if you want someone perfect. . ."

"I don't know if I want him at all; we're so different."

"You sure were awfully worried about him a while back."

"That's because it's dangerous. I would have felt that way about anyone about to go into a forest fire," she rationalized.

"I know, I know," Red nodded.

Kelly turned her attention to looking for road signs to guide her back to town. In spite of Steven's abandoning her so suddenly, leaving her to find her way home, to rearrange the promotion, she couldn't help admiring him. How could she be angry for long at someone who was willing to risk his life for others? It was one thing to jump in front of spectators and enjoy the tribute of the crowd, but quite another to behave heroically when no one else would even see or hear of it.

A question from Red interrupted her reverie. "I'm sorry," she apologized, "my thoughts were wandering. What did you ask?"

"I said, you don't think I'm too old, do you?"

"Too old for what?"

"To get back into skydiving."

Kelly looked at him, puzzled. "I don't know, Red. I know so little about it. I guess if you were just starting for the first time, people might think so, but you've done it before. You're experienced."

"That's right," he said forcefully. "It won't take me long to practice up a bit. I'm not worried about forgetting anything, but I'd do a little practicing on the jump stands just to get the feel of it. I might even jump with Steven at Fairmount, especially now that it's been delayed. How long will it be delayed, do you think?"

"I don't know!" Distressed again over the situation, she remained silent as they finished the trip, her thoughts again on the man who had brought her to this predicament. *Oh, Steven,* she thought, *you may be a hero, all right, but you certainly have a knack for making my life uncomfortable!*

nine

Kelly found her life suddenly cheerless, repetitive, and frustrating. As she waited for Steven at the airfield, the sullen, overcast sky matched her mood.

In the two weeks since he had rushed off to fight the forest fire, she had been more than occupied with the necessary paperwork connected with the tour. Everything that had been done before had to be undone and new arrangements made. The entire schedule had to be shifted, with Kelly making numerous telephone calls, trying to soothe irate heads of charitable groups, airport managers, skydiving club officials, and countless others.

Work had never depressed her before; she had always considered herself a very organized person, one who enjoyed attention to details. *This is ridiculous,* she told herself. Yet in the back of her mind she knew that her sudden discontent was not wholly the result of the tension of shifting plans and the extra work it entailed. Lyle had become another problem in her life; perhaps that accounted for her dismal mood.

The change in plans had allowed Kelly to remain in town, and Lyle had taken advantage of her presence in the office to invite her out several times. She refused all these invitations, but she was running out of plausible excuses and still could not bring herself to give the explanation that would keep Lyle from continuing his attentions.

That explanation, of course, was her growing love for Steven. Having once seen the light and broken the barrier of her prejudice, she now admitted to herself that she admired everything about him. No longer did she consider skydiving the ultimate stupidity. No longer did she cringe at the thought of spending her life with someone who taught people how to parachute. After meeting so many skydivers in recent weeks, she realized it wasn't as dangerous a sport as she first believed—and no less worthy an endeavor than the one she herself pursued. After all, skydiving was a form of show business, as well as a sport. And she, as a promotion manager, put on shows.

But what about a nice home, stable environment, and children? Well, skydivers certainly had wives and children; she had met them. Most of the men were weekend jumpers, though, spending their days at regular steady jobs. But not Steven. Skydiving occupied his entire life. And what about her commitment to Christ, a commitment he did not share? She realized now that she could not try to change him into anyone else; she either had to accept him as he was or leave him alone. Oh, but how could she leave Steven? Somehow, insidiously, he had established a place in her heart, and now she was overwhelmed by the thought of the end of the promotion and the possibility of never seeing him again.

And how did Steven think about her? He had made the first overtures regarding their relationship. He said he cared for her, kissed her fervently on so many occasions. Was he ready for a commitment to her? If he would only open his heart to Christ, she would gladly commit herself to him—but he suddenly seemed aloof and distant.

She had not seen him since the fire claimed his attention, but they had spoken once on the telephone. At that time, he spoke briefly, almost curtly, then apologized, saying he had something on his mind. They had handled their business and hung up.

On Sunday Kelly had attended church as usual, and once again she saw Christopher Trask enter on his butler's arm, sit in the rear, and leave quickly afterward.

Pastor Wallace had come up to her as she stood staring after Steven's father. "Hello, Kelly. I saw you looking toward Mr. Trask. Do you know him?"

"A little. Does he come here often?"

"He seems to be returning to us, I'm happy to say. His late wife was our dear and faithful worker, but after she died, the family stopped attending. Their son attended our church school, and perhaps he will also return to the Lord one day."

"Perhaps." Kelly wanted to ask about Steven's church school days, but other people wanted to speak to the pastor.

Now, as Steven's long strides covered the strip of grass on the airfield, she saw he wore a tense, worried look. But when he stopped in front of her, his face softened. She moved close to him and looked into his eyes. "I've missed you. We've barely spoken since you came back. What's the matter?"

"I can't talk about it just now." His voice was tight, although he stroked her shoulders tenderly.

Her stomach threatening to tie itself into knots, Kelly cringed. That same excuse. He made it sound as if some deep, dark secret resided in his soul, something so terrible that nothing could surmount it. She trembled.

"It's not you," he said, holding her by both arms and looking deeply into her eyes. "I didn't want to fall in love with you—but I have."

Sudden tears brimmed in her eyes. "Oh, Steven, I've longed to hear you say that. I love you too." Her heart pounding, she stretched on tiptoe and put her arms around him, her lips seeking his. As they kissed, she couldn't help thinking what a strange time and place he had chosen for his declaration. People were probably watching them, although she didn't care.

His tender kiss became more possessive for a moment, but just as suddenly, he relaxed and released her. "Oh, Kelly," he said. "I want you so much. You have to be patient with me, though. I have a lot to learn."

"You can have all the time you need," she murmured.

A squeeze of her shoulders was his only response, and he led her across the tarmac. Once more a frown furrowed his forehead, and he said, almost brusquely, "Why did you encourage Red to take up skydiving again?"

"But I didn't." She was surprised by the accusation.

He stopped walking and turned to her. "He said you told him to go ahead."

Kelly felt under attack and backed up instinctively, trying to remember her conversation with Red. "I said that since he had been a skydiver once, he probably could get back into it without too much difficulty. I didn't encourage him. He asked my opinion and that's all I said. Steven, what's the matter?"

"He's too old for the sport. I'm thinking of giving it up myself—and I'm thirty years younger!"

"Give it up?" Kelly repeated his words breathlessly. Was that what had been troubling him? But why did he want to—was it for her? Did he think he would please her if he did? A thousand questions sprang to her lips.

"You can't do this kind of thing forever," he said. "Your reflexes have to be sharp; it takes tremendous physical stamina."

"I realize that, but why should what I say have an influence on Red? I had the feeling he had already made up his mind before he asked me. Even if I had said it was a foolish idea, he wouldn't have listened."

"He wants you to look up to him, to admire him."

She stammered, "But of course I do. We've become friends. But I know almost nothing about skydiving. Why should he care what I think about that?"

"Ever since you came around, he's been like an adoring puppy, following you around, practically worshipping you."

"Steven, do you realize what you're saying?"

He dropped his head and a heavy breath escaped his lips. "I'm jealous of Red." He lifted his head and smiled at her. "I guess I've never had such a terrible case of love before."

She hugged him, feeling the smooth tight fabric of his jumpsuit against her cheek. "I've been the same way, remember, about your little cousin."

"But I'm still worried about Red," Steven resumed. "He's been practicing every day for the last two weeks. He bought some used equipment and is all set to jump today!" He flung the words at her as if in frustration.

"I don't see why you're so worried," Kelly argued. "You're the jumpmaster. If you don't want him to jump, tell him. He has to obey you, doesn't he? Aren't you in charge?"

"He does everything right," Steven said, irritated. "There's really no way I can stop him, no technical way. And he's my friend besides. How can I deny him?"

Kelly heart again went out to him. She couldn't help admiring his obvious concern for his friend.

"But if he does it correctly," Kelly said, "why are you worried? He told me has thousands of jumps to his credit."

"Years ago, yes. This is now!"

"Has he passed a recent physical?"

"Yes, I told you there's really no reason for me to stop him." He thrust one hand through his thick black hair and heaved a sigh. "Forget it," he added. "I suppose I'm being foolish. I'm on edge, that's all."

Kelly touched his arm, wanting to soothe him. In the distance she heard the revving of airplane engines and knew time was short. "It will be all right, you'll see. I think it's the weather. This gloomy day is making us all dispirited. We'll feel better when the sun comes out."

"I wish it were only that." He gave her a half smile. "I have to get back to the hangar." Then he turned and left.

Kelly now found his worry transferred to her; she too liked Red and wanted him safe. But surely he would be; he had never been happier than the last few days, anticipating his first jump after nine years. And he had experience, after all. She tried to chase her gloom by such reasoning, but it refused to depart.

&

The sun still had not appeared when the meet began. The spectators filled the bleachers, the band played, yet Kelly remained as downcast as before. Steven said he loved her—surely that ought to override everything—yet a gnawing worry continued. She watched from the sidelines as the skydivers did their maneuvers in midair, opened their chutes, and landed.

Because of the low-hanging clouds, the planes did not go as high as usual, and the jumpers were clearly visible. They had much less time to do their stunts before pulling the rip cord. She felt as if she had seen it all a hundred times before, and the thrill it once evoked seemed lacking. Yet she knew it was a temporary malaise on her part. It would pass.

Then Red jumped. Her boredom vanished; her heart seemed to leap into her throat and stay there. He did a front loop, then a backloop. The loops were ragged, but acceptable. He was not up there, after all, to win a prize. One more backloop and then he'd pull the rip cord.

But something was wrong. He looked out of control. Instead of arms outstretched in stable position, one hand pressed against his chest. Kelly thought he was going to pull the rip cord, yet she knew his placement was wrong. Down, down he came, his hand never moving from his chest.

Kelly jumped up and ran to the edge of the field. "Pull the rip cord!" she screamed aloud, and then realized her rashness. The band, which had been doing a low drum roll, waiting to burst into a fanfare when the chute opened, stopped playing altogether. A hum of excited voices came from the stands. Other people stood, staring as she was into the sky.

Just when Kelly thought she could stand it no more, the pack on Red's chest erupted, and a small parachute blossomed into life. He had pulled the emergency chute instead of the main one! But he was too close to the ground. No, not the ground, the hangar. He had done nothing to place himself over the field and time had run out. His body made two oscillations and then slammed into the hangar and fell the remaining fifteen feet to the ground.

The field exploded into action, everyone moving at once. The M.C. tried vainly to keep people in their seats, shouting into his microphone, but he was ignored. Kelly reached Red's side almost at once, but Gary Nelson, who had completed his jump, blocked her way and grabbed her roughly by the shoulders.

"You don't want to see him," he growled. "Stay back.

Get the people back in their seats. I'll handle this."

Once more her obligations took precedence, and Kelly, breathing all but suspended, heart racing, turned around and staggered back to the others, urging them to go back to their seats, yelling for the security guards to help.

Chaos reigned on the field for almost half an hour before order was finally restored. Red was taken into the hangar, the doors closed, and the spectators, deprived of anything to watch, gradually returned to the bleachers, and the exhibition continued. Then the M.C. announced that Red Johnson was alive and being taken to the hospital; moments afterward, an ambulance arrived, remained briefly, and departed again.

Kelly sat in a daze for the rest of the afternoon, torn between wanting to go to the hospital and her attention to duty. The day had been spoiled for everyone, and after watching a few more jumps, the crowd dispersed. Nothing a skydiver did after that could equal the heart-stopping excitement of Red's fall.

Through it all, Kelly had not seen Steven. He did not make his jump, and she did not see him in the crush after the accident. Lethargically, she wandered around the field, watching the cleanup crews, talking to other parachutists, pilots, and friends. When everyone else had gone, she remained, unable to summon the energy to walk to her car. Now that she could logically leave the field and go to the hospital, she felt reluctant, wanting to postpone the moment when she might hear bad news.

She wandered into the hangar again and this time noticed the parachute on the floor. It was Red's, the one he had pulled at the last moment. It looked like a silky bed sheet thrown in a heap. She sat down on it, touching its folds with shaking fingers. She almost imagined she could keep him alive by holding onto the chute itself; then she dismissed the thought, and simply prayed. After a long time, she lay down on the nylon fabric, not stretching out, but turning on her side and bringing her knees up, hugging them with her arms, as if rolling into a ball would keep out the terrible memory of what had happened to her friend.

Incredibly, she slept. The traumatic events of the day had taken their toll, and the next thing she heard was a car driving up and stopping, its engine cut abruptly. Then silence for a moment until the door of the hangar slid open, screeching on its tracks. Her eyes sprang open and the darkness of the huge room surprised her. She must have slept for hours. She turned and twisted to a sitting position and peered into the gloom to identify the owner of the heavy footsteps on the floor. In a moment, Steven stood over her.

"Kelly," he said, as if surprised. "I see we're both drawn to the scene of the crime." He laughed bitterly at his own phrase.

"How is Red?" she asked at once. She would have risen, but Steven sank down beside her, resting his arms on his upraised knees and lowering his head between them wearily.

"He's alive," he mumbled.

"Thank God," she whispered. "What happened? Why didn't he open his main chute? Is he badly hurt?"

Steven raised his head. "He had a heart attack in midair."

"A heart attack? But the physical? You said he had just had a physical."

"That's what I asked the doctors too. In fact, I probably shouted it at them. How could they let this happen to Red? It's a miracle he's still alive. Somehow he realized he didn't have time for the main chute and pulled the reserve instead. He's in critical condition, but they won't say more until morning."

Kelly touched his arm. "Steven, he'll be all right. I know he will."

"Why did this happen?" Steven demanded. "Why him?"

"We don't know why some things happen, but we can't blame anyone."

"But I do," he said, his voice rising in pitch. "I blame the doctors. I blame Red for trying to jump at his age. Most of all I blame myself. I shouldn't have let him go."

"You couldn't know this would happen."

"I knew, somehow I knew. I told you this afternoon, didn't I? I had a dread of his jumping, but I couldn't find a legal reason to stop him. Just my intuition. But I should have listened to that." He pounded his fist into his knee with such force that Kelly flinched as if she could feel the blow.

She knew she mustn't let him go on blaming himself. "It's not your fault," she repeated. "Accidents can happen to anyone. You did the right thing. Why, only a week ago Red told me you were the best jumpmaster he'd ever seen, that your jumpers abide by the rules and you have the best safety record in the state."

"It wasn't enough," Steven railed, his voice cracking. He pressed his palms to his closed eyes, as if trying to blot out the image of the fall. Silence surrounded them while Steven choked back tears, and Kelly searched her mind for something helpful to say.

"It's this stupid business," he said finally, speaking in a lower tone as if to himself. "What am I doing here? Holding the lives of all these people in my hands?"

"That's not true," Kelly insisted. "You didn't force anyone to become a skydiver, certainly not Red. He made jumps when you were a child. People know the risks before they start, and you, of all people, have probably saved dozens of lives by proper teaching and insisting on safety measures."

"Don't try to exonerate me," he said in a desolate voice. "I should never have started this in the first place. I tried to prove something, and now look what I've done. My father was right—I couldn't accept being second to anyone. I had to be first, the best. And now I've almost killed my best friend."

After another pause, he continued, and Kelly didn't interrupt him; she knew he must pour out his anger and frustration, talking to himself more than to her. And perhaps talking would help him come to terms with this tragedy—and with the demons that held him prisoner, the ones he refused to discuss. Perhaps now, at last, Christ would be able to lay His healing hand on Steven's heart.

"My father was successful and wanted me to take over his business. At first I was willing—but then I began telling him how to do things, thinking I knew it all. What a laugh! My worst stupidity was leaving. We had a terrible quarrel and I left him and his business and never went back. I was going to show him! I was going to be the best at whatever I chose, and that's what I did. I loved having my name in the newspapers and on television; I hoped my father would see it. I won all the skydiving contests. I've done just what my father did, but in a different field. I conquered the sport, and for what? To prove something that didn't need proving. I didn't need to compete with my father, and now look what I've done! Red was like a second father to me—I guess that's why I love him so. I substituted him for the one I turned my back on."

Tears slid down Kelly's cheeks, and she put her arm around Steven's shoulders, trying to let him know she shared his anguish and sorrow. "It's not too late," she said softly. "Red's still alive, and so is your father. I'm sure he forgave you long ago and is just waiting for you to come back so he can tell you."

"I can't go to my father. You don't understand. It's not just that I turned my back on his business. I said such terrible things to him. I accused him of murdering my mother."

Kelly's breath caught in her throat. "Murdering. . . ?"

"I don't mean really murdering. I mean I blamed him for her death. I wasn't there, you see, and I thought if he hadn't sent me away to school, there would have been something I could do."

"At sixteen? Steven, you were just upset. It was perfectly natural to feel that way. But I'm sure your father did everything possible for your mother. He loved her."

"Did he? Or did he love his precious business more?"

"You don't really feel that way?"

"I don't know what I think anymore. He was so much older than I. I always felt such awe of him. I couldn't speak to him like boys usually speak to their fathers."

"He probably regrets that as much as you do."

"There was only my mother, and when she died I blamed him. Every year I hated him more—until finally I left. But leaving didn't bring satisfaction. Not even being the best skydiver did that. Oh, Kelly, you don't know the many ways I've tried to blot out the constant pain inside."

"Only God's grace can truly help."

"But don't you see? God was to blame for all of this! God made my father too old to be a real companion to me. God took my mother when I was young!"

"So it isn't your father you blame, but God."

Steven looked into her eyes, questioning, searching. "Why

did He let my mother die? Why did He let Red fall?"

"We don't know God's plan. All I know is that when I trust God completely, then good things come into my life."

"I don't understand what you're saying." Steven wiped a hand across his face. "But I do know that I've made a mess of my life. Why do some people take so long to grow up?"

"I can't answer all your questions," Kelly said. "You need to talk to someone else, to trust God—"

"I don't know God, so I can't trust Him." He got to his feet and looked away. "I'm not worthy of you, any more than I am of Red, or my father. Good-bye, Kelly." He backed away as he spoke, then turned and strode from the hangar.

"Steven!" Kelly called, but she knew he wasn't listening, even if he could hear her. Soon his car started and drove off. With a cry of anguish, she threw herself down onto the parachute again, feeling its hard fabric burn her elbows. Sobs wracked her body, and her cries echoed through the hollow building.

ten

Steven could not be found. He was not at his apartment nor the airport nor even in the hospital visiting Red. Whenever Kelly went there herself, she would ask if anyone had seen the skydiver, but she always received "no" for an answer. If he came to visit his friend, he did it like a thief and went undetected.

Kelly had not tried to contact Steven the first day after the accident, reasoning he needed time to recover somewhat, and that if he wanted to see her, he'd call. But gradually she realized the seriousness of his absence, and she set about finding him. Intruding upon her grief and worry were feelings of responsibility for the tour and the exhibitions. She had, of course, told Lyle about the accident, and at first he was very understanding, telling her to postpone the next event until everyone had recovered from the shock.

But recovery proceeded slowly. At the airport, activity all but halted. Red had been more than the airport manager, the trusted friend and driving force behind operations at the field; he had been a fixture, someone who seemed always to be there. Even men who had not been flying for many years couldn't remember when Red Johnson hadn't been around. Without him nothing ran smoothly, and the uncertainty of his recovery shrouded every day with lethargy. People stood around the hangar, talking in muffled tones, wondering when, or if, Red would be back.

And now, Steven too had disappeared from the airport. Depressed, Kelly stopped going there, telephoning instead

138

in her constant efforts to find him. Every day brought the same report: he had not been seen; no one knew his whereabouts.

Then a week later, Christopher Trask called, telling her he had arranged for funding the opera promotion. The news, which should have overjoyed her, made little difference. Previously she would have been happy to be free of the skydiving exhibition; now its demise held no joy for her. She had not wanted it to end like this, with Red injured, Steven vanished, and her newly-found love a burning, hard knot in the pit of her stomach.

Still, she knew she must carry on. If Steven couldn't be found, and he certainly seemed to have totally disappeared, then the skydiving promotion would terminate, she would do the opera benefit, and somehow she'd survive.

Lyle, however, took the situation almost as badly as Kelly. "How opportune," he said one morning, standing in her office. "The skydiving promotion is postponed because the head man has conveniently run off, and that leaves you free to do what you've preferred from the beginning."

Kelly was surprised at the sarcasm in his tone, and she felt her face become tight and drawn. "That's not fair, Lyle." She longed to tell him how terribly Steven's disappearance affected her. He was concerned about a mere promotion; she had lost the man she loved. And now she could never tell Lyle the truth. "You did promise me," she reminded him, "that I could have the opera promotion whenever the funds became available. Well, now they have. Steven's sudden withdrawal has nothing to do with that."

"What am I to do about the charities that were lined up for the remaining events? How can I explain to all those people?"

"I'm sure you'll handle it; you'll find someone else to

take it over."

"But how can anyone take it over when the star is gone?"

"I'm sure he'll turn up eventually. Perhaps someone else will have better luck finding him than I did."

"I don't see how anyone else could do it if you can't," he said. "After all, he's probably in love with you."

Kelly felt her face flush, and the pain inside, which she'd been trying to conquer, came again to torture her. "That's not true," she answered, afraid she meant it. Steven had apparently *not* been in love with her, or he wouldn't leave her like this. Why, she asked herself again, did he not call?

Lyle came around her desk and looked down at her. Her gaze dropped to her desk, trying to hide the tears that sprang to her eyes. Lyle's voice softened, and he put his hands on her shoulders and raised her to her feet.

"I'm sorry," he said. "I didn't mean to take my frustration out on you. You're right—you're not to blame for this. It's my responsibility, always has been. And I did promise you could quit the promotion, so I guess I'll have to handle it somehow."

Kelly looked up at him. "I'll be glad to help. I never intended to leave you in a predicament."

"No, it's not your fault. It's that crazy skydiver—he's irresponsible and egotistical—hiding out somewhere, leaving us to manage alone, failing to live up to his part of the bargain."

Kelly wanted to contradict him, to swear that Steven was a fine, loyal, conscientious person, but she couldn't bring herself to utter the words. They seemed false in light of this evidence that he had simply run away rather than fulfill his obligations.

Lyle put his arms around Kelly. "I could never rebuke you at any rate. You know I'm falling in love with you."

Kelly had known in some remote corner of her mind that Lyle would continue to press his case, but surely he couldn't mean this. "Lyle," she began, trying to pull away from him, "we haven't known each other long."

"Long enough," he answered. "Oh, you've been putting me off, but I'm not going to go away. I know we're meant for each other, and I'm sure that—once we have a chance to spend more time together—you'll see it too. You're going to have dinner with me every night, until you realize that." He grinned like a man convinced of his eventual success.

Kelly again tried to free herself from his arms. "Please, Lyle, someone might come in."

"Let them. I'd like the whole office to know how I feel."

Unable to back up further because of the chair, she could only protest weakly. "Lyle, please. I can't talk about it now."

"Promise me you'll go to dinner with me tonight."

"I can't."

"At least think about it."

"I'll think about it." She would say anything at this point to get him to release her, but he leaned forward to kiss her.

His lips were almost on hers when the door to her office suddenly opened, and the mail girl entered. "Oh, excuse me," she said, a blush creeping up her face. "I'm just bringing the mail." With that, she dropped a collection of letters on the desk and left hastily.

Kelly used the interruption to break from Lyle's grasp. She turned quickly and reached for the mail. "I really must get back to work." She sifted through the envelopes, glancing at the return addresses.

Lyle, instead of renewing his assault, stood meekly behind her, watching, until he suddenly said, "Stop! What's that?" He took an envelope from her hand. "It's from the Awards Committee," he exclaimed, and tore it open, unfolding the single sheet of paper inside.

Kelly, meanwhile, had been attracted to a different envelope. It had no return address at all, but the handwriting, bold and upright, commanded her attention. Not bothering to reach for her letter opener, she thrust a fingernail into the edge of the flap and ripped it aside. A check fell out, but she let it drop and read the few words on the accompanying page.

"Dear Miss Marsh," it read. "I regret I am unable to continue in your skydiving exhibitions. Please accept the enclosed check, which is the return of my fee, and my apologies. I am giving up skydiving and leaving the area. Below are the names of two people who could take my place. Steven Barry."

Kelly dropped heavily into the chair, letting the paper fall to the desk, where Lyle retrieved it and read it aloud. "Well," he commented, "I guess he has a sense of decency after all."

"Yes, a sense of decency," Kelly repeated, her face tightening and tears threatening to erupt.

Lyle flung the letter down and placed on top the one he had been reading first. "But look at this," he said brightly. "The day isn't a total loss after all."

Kelly looked, but the words blurred under her gaze. "What does it say?" she asked.

"You've won," Lyle announced jubilantly. "Your sports promotion at the Park Side Mall, the one you didn't want to do," he added with emphasis, "has won first prize in the original events category. The Valley Promotion Managers, at their ceremony next month, will award you the statuette, the Archie!"

Conflicting emotions raced through Kelly as she heard the latest news. In only her second year as a promotion director, she had won the coveted Archie award. Tears broke at last and cascaded down her face, and she let them fall, not caring who saw them. The award meant nothing. Steven was gone forever.

ea

The next few weeks were even busier for Kelly, if that were possible, than the preceding ones had been. Although the paperwork and forms had lessened, the opera benefit entailed far more in the way of telephone calls and personal visits.

Each evening she collapsed into bed, weary to her very bones, yet realizing that the tired feelings were as much the result of her depressed mood as her work. She found herself desperate for sleep as soon as she finished dinner, yawning and scarcely able to keep her eyes open. Then she'd sleep soundly until the clock radio woke her the next morning.

Occasionally she let Lyle take her to dinner or to a film, but these dates only increased her feeling of being constantly tired. She had little desire to be with Lyle. After Steven, everyone else seemed bland and uninteresting. Yet she let her head tell her that since she couldn't have Steven, she might as well get over him as quickly as possible. She could do worse in the way of a husband than Lyle, whose ambition would probably take him far. She did not let herself think about whether he shared her relationship with God; she did not want to think at all. For now, she only endured the days.

The awards ceremony was scheduled for the first week of September, and she and Lyle drove to San Francisco together early in the day. Although she'd been to the city several times before, she let Lyle play tour guide, and they rode the cable cars up California Street, drove the winding turns of Lombard, visited the quaint shops in Ghiradelli Square, and even went up to Telegraph Hill and looked out at the sailboats on the bay.

At six P.M., they arrived at the Sheraton-Palace Hotel and went directly to the rooms provided by the awards committee. Kelly changed into a long gown of turquoise silk, with hand-painted flowers and butterflies extending from just above her waist on the left side down the entire straight length of the skirt and around the border of the hem. The dress had spaghetti-thin straps, but she had a shawl of the same fabric to throw over her shoulders, and her silk shoes had been dyed to match. Her blond hair, brushed to a shiny mane, framed her face, its waves nestling around her neck, and her only jewelry was a small strand of pearls that had been in her family for years. When Lyle saw her, his sharp intake of breath told her the effect was perfect, and she shoved to the back of her mind the sudden longing to have Steven be the man standing before her.

Together with other promotion managers, many of whom Kelly knew, they entered the breathtaking Garden Court ballroom, its vaulted ceiling topped with leaded glass windows, its many chandeliers sparkling, and found seats at the round tables. Everyone had dressed especially for the occasion: the ladies in formal gowns, the men in tuxedos. Like so many of the events they promoted, this too benefitted charity, and besides the firms and their employees, there were also a large number of prominent society people from the bay area. Lyle pointed out a famous columnist from the San Francisco *Chronicle,* and she recognized a well-known society woman at a nearby table.

The dinner was lavish, but Kelly could eat very little, being both nervous and upset. Although Red was progressing well in the hospital, and she had been assured on her latest visit that he would be walking soon, she still could not shake the depression that clung to her every waking moment.

Nothing in the program which followed did anything to alleviate her mood. The program consisted of speeches by members of the Promotion Managers Association and the various charities which benefitted, plus film clips of the promotions that were going to be acknowledged. When scenes of her own promotion came on the screen, Kelly was startled to see how good it looked, but she felt no pride. Finally the lights went up again, and several pretty girls carried the silver statuettes—the Archies—to a table near the microphone.

Kelly used the intermission to find a powder room. To her surprise, her face looked serene, giving no hint of the turmoil inside. Once more, she walked across the thick carpet toward the glass ballroom doors. Then suddenly a familiar face emerged from the crowd of people returning to their tables. Steven.

Seconds passed as she stood frozen in front of him. He seemed different dressed in a black dinner jacket, though it looked as natural on him as his usual jumpsuit. Every dark hair of his head lay perfectly in place, his eyes seemed bluer than ever, and his lips curved up as if with some pleasant secret. For long moments they stared at each other, and then Kelly leaned into him as if her body had a will of its own. Steven's arms went around her, and he held her close, murmuring her name against her hair. Then he pulled her into a corner and held her at arms' length, looking appreciatively at her costume.

"You are absolutely gorgeous," he said, "although I've always thought so, even in that secondhand yellow jumpsuit you wore to ground school."

Kelly laughed. "You look pretty gorgeous yourself. How did you know I was here? Where have you been? I've been frantic!"

"Hold on a minute," he said. "All in good time. I have so much to tell you. I called the other day but missed you. Then I read about this in the newspaper and came here instead. I can't wait to tell you my news. I owe you an apology too."

"What news?" Kelly's agony of the past weeks evaporated and she reveled in his looks and his words. Nothing really mattered except his return and the fact that he apparently still loved her. They would work out everything else. "Can you tell me now? Come and sit at my table. Are you really giving up skydiving?"

"There you go again," he protested, his voice teasing. "No, I can't sit at your table. I brought my cousin Hayley. She loves dress-up events but she's always late, and this was my first chance to get you alone."

"You could have come to my table—"

"No, I must talk to you privately."

"I'm ready. Just tell me when and where—and soon, please."

Steven's eyes narrowed, and his smile vanished. Kelly turned her head to see what had disturbed him. Lyle was striding purposefully toward her.

"Kelly, why are you hiding here? The awards are on right now!" Apparently not recognizing Steven, Lyle ignored him and pulled her toward the ballroom. "It's your turn!"

"I'll see you later," Steven called to her, and she let Lyle lead her back, her heart pounding, feeling alternately too cold and too hot. She thought her face must be flushed, yet her lips felt frozen. Lyle headed for the podium and she realized she had not even collected her thoughts about what she would say.

The lights seemed unbearably bright, and she felt every eye on her as she allowed Lyle to escort her to the front of the room. The president of the association made a brief speech and then put the silver figure into her trembling hands. Its smooth surface cold under her fingers, its weight surprising her, she glanced at it for some moments before smiling to the audience and approaching the microphone. She made a brief acceptance speech, words tumbling out quickly; she remembered to thank Lyle, telling the audience that he deserved the award since he had insisted she do the sports promotion, a new field for her.

The room vibrated with applause, after which Lyle went to the microphone and thanked Kelly. Then, putting his arm around her shoulder and drawing her to his side, he added, "You all know her as an exceptional director—but I also know her as a special woman, not only beautiful and talented, but compassionate as well." He paused, then added almost as an afterthought, "In fact, I hope one day she will consent to be my wife."

The spectators, apparently thrilled by this announcement, applauded even more loudly, some of them actually getting to their feet to clap, but Kelly could only stand and stare. What had he done? Why had he said such a thing? And in front of all these people? In front of Steven!

Tears of rage and embarrassment sprang to her eyes, but she fought them down, smiling a broad false smile and trying to retreat from all the stares and attention. Still nodding and smiling, she walked past the many other tables, searching the crowd through clouded vision for Steven's face, until she reached her chair and sank into it, feeling weak and almost nauseous.

She must find Steven, but her legs trembled, and she couldn't regain her feet. She put the heavy statuette on the table and tried to rise, but Lyle sat down next to her and held her arm. She turned brimming eyes to him, saying in a stage whisper, "Why did you do that? How could you. . . ?"

"But it's true. I do want to marry you. Just because you haven't said 'yes' yet—"

"Did you think you could make it impossible for me to say anything else just by announcing it?"

"Darling, you must say yes," he pleaded, his face intense.

Kelly turned away from him, fumbling in her bag for a handkerchief, staring unseeing at the people who began to crowd around the table, congratulating them as if her marriage to Lyle were an accomplished fact.

"Lyle is a little premature," she said to a woman who gushed over them. By now she had managed to rise but could not move forward for the crush. "There's nothing definite," she said to a man who kissed her on the cheek in a burst of enthusiasm. In spite of her anger and concern, she could not bring herself to publicly humiliate Lyle by calling him a liar. Besides, the only important thing was finding Steven.

"Congratulations on your award," he said in his husky voice, and Kelly's heart stopped. How had he suddenly appeared? What must he think? Surely he didn't believe she cared for Lyle. He couldn't think she'd agree to marry someone else just because he'd been gone for a few weeks.

"Steven, let me explain—"

"Oh, by the way, congratulations on your engagement. I

hope you'll be very happy."

"But I'm not engaged," she blurted, putting her hand out to him, touching the edge of his sleeve. "Lyle shouldn't have. . .I don't know why he said that. . ."

"You don't have to explain," he said quickly. "I don't blame you for wanting someone less impetuous and thoughtless."

"But I do have to explain. Steven, please listen to me."

"There's nothing more to say. I was wrong about you. I've been wrong before. I'll get over it." His jaw tight, he turned and vanished into the crowd as quickly as he had materialized.

Kelly clung to the back of her chair, stiffening the muscles in her legs, willing them not to send her crumpling to the floor. Another crowd of well-wishers faced her, saying things she didn't want to hear. This time she didn't even attempt to answer. She simply stood still and prayed for strength, strength to do what she must do, or strength to bear the loss of Steven forever.

eleven

Gravel crunching under her tires, Kelly wound her way up the driveway to the Trask house. Morning sun glinted off the windows, and the air felt fresh and clean, although slightly chilly. When the butler answered her ring, he said, "Mr. Trask is expecting you," and led her to the living room.

As before, Christopher Trask did not rise from his chair. In fact, although he gave her a pleasant smile, he seemed more frail than previously. His skin had a grayish quality, and his features stood out more prominently.

"Thank you for coming," he said, extending a fragile hand.

"Not at all," she replied. Kelly's stomach knotted, as it had when she first read his message on the pink slip of paper her secretary had handed her. She wondered about his reason for seeing her this morning. Her first thought had been that he wanted to withdraw his support of the opera benefit and didn't want to break such bad news over the telephone. Why else would he request a personal meeting? On the long drive to his home, she had come up with no better excuse. Even the possibility that he wanted to discuss details of the promotion didn't strike her as plausible. That could have been done by telephone. She had, after all, come on short notice.

Putting speculation aside, she reminded herself that she would soon know, and she sat in the chair near his side while they discussed the weather.

"Actually," Trask said finally, a frown creasing his high forehead, "my health is not what I could wish. My doctors tell me I shall require an immediate operation."

"Oh, I'm so sorry to hear that," Kelly said. "Not a serious one, I hope?"

"Serious enough," he answered and then paused.

"Surgery is very advanced these days," Kelly added. "I'm sure you'll be just fine."

"Perhaps," he said. "At any rate, I didn't call you here to complain about it, although what I'm going to ask is related."

"Related? How?"

"My illness has caused me to do a lot of thinking lately, and I've finally come to the realization that I may not live forever." He gave a soft, dry chuckle, and Kelly's heart went out to him that he could still make jokes about it.

"I suppose we all come to this point sometime," he went on. "I've been very fortunate to have such a long and relatively healthy life. But surgery is never completely without risk and when one is of advanced years, one must expect the odds to drop."

"I'm sure the doctors wouldn't have suggested the operation if they didn't feel you'd benefit from it."

"Oh, yes, they do give me every assurance I'll survive it, but I have another reason for my worry."

"What's that?"

"The break with my son has bothered me more and more lately, and I think I can't rule out the possibility it affects my health. While I'm so worried about this, I'm not a very good patient—and, furthermore, if I don't recover, I can't meet my Maker without first having reconciled with my son."

Kelly paused before speaking. Although the thought had

crossed her mind to try to find Steven through his father, she had rejected it. After their many years of estrangement, she had no reason to think he had suddenly contacted his father now. Still, perhaps Mr. Trask did know something. "I think reconciliation is a very good thing," she said, waiting to hear what Trask would say about Steven.

"The problem is," he went on, "I don't know where he is. I used to know; I thought I could reach him quickly if I really needed to. He didn't know that, of course," Trask added. "But now he's suddenly disappeared and the private detectives I hired haven't a clue to his whereabouts. I have no doubt they'll find him eventually, but I can't wait much longer. The doctors are urging this operation on me, and I've already delayed them a week. You've been working with him. Do you know where he is?"

"I don't think I can help you," Kelly said. "I haven't seen him in weeks, no one has." This was a small lie, but she had tried to blot out their painful meeting at the awards dinner.

"But you will try, won't you?" his father asked, leaning forward and entreating her with his eyes, his hands reaching out to clasp hers. "You know these skydivers and can get information that perhaps the detectives can't. I'm sure they'll track him down in time, but time is growing short for me. I'll pay you, of course, the same rate I pay the detectives. Oh, please say yes."

"I wouldn't dream of accepting payment," Kelly said. "I've been looking for him too." She paused; she had never said this before. "You see, I'm in love with your son. I thought he loved me too, but evidently I was mistaken."

The old man's expression went through a series of changes, ending with a smile. "Thank you for telling me, my dear. I'm sure it wasn't easy. And please learn from my mistakes. Don't give up on him as I once did. If you find him, you will earn the undying gratitude of an old, foolish man." He sat back in his chair again and closed his eyes while he spoke. "I should never have allowed this to happen in the first place, much less let it continue so long."

"I'm sure you did your best," she said.

"No, not really. Oh, at first, I was all in the right and he in the wrong—but that is small consolation to me now. I'm the one who should have broken the long silence. I was older and supposedly wiser. I should have told him years ago that I had forgiven him and wanted only his happiness."

"People are not always as wise as they should be. We're only human, after all."

Trask opened his eyes again and smiled weakly at Kelly. "I never prayed enough when my wife was so ill—but I'll not make the same mistake twice. Between my praying and your searching, perhaps I'll see my son's face once more."

"You will, I promise," Kelly said, "I've seen you at my church services, and I'll be praying too."

He smiled. "I feel more hopeful already."

"But I must tell you that I can't think of another place he might be that I haven't looked already. Except. . ."

"Yes?"

"Maybe your niece Hayley knows where to find Steven." Kelly related the bare facts of her encounter with Steven at the awards banquet two days earlier.

"Of course I can give you Hayley's number. Oh, what a scatterbrain that girl is. She should have told me she had seen him so recently."

"Don't blame her. She may not realize Steven is missing.

I'll call her now, if I may."

Using the telephone in a niche under the hall stairs, Kelly dialed the number Trask gave her, praying that Hayley would be there and that she'd know Steven's whereabouts. Unfortunately, although Hayley was at home, she had no idea where he could be.

"He called last week and asked if I wanted to go to a fancy dinner party for charity and I did—but then when the dull part was over and I wanted to stay and dance, he dragged me home."

"Thanks anyway, Hayley. If you hear from him again, please tell him to call his father immediately. It's urgent."

When she returned to Trask's side with the news, the man sighed heavily. "Thank you again. You must excuse me now. If I'm to postpone the operation for another week, I must rest and not aggravate my condition any further. You must call me the moment you hear anything—and I shall call you as well."

Kelly squeezed his hand and then turned to go.

Trask's voice stopped her once more. "You are such a lovely person," he added. "I don't wonder my son fell in love with you. You look exactly as I would wish a daughter-in-law to look: golden and full of light and warmth. I could have such lovely grandchildren. . ." His voice trailed off and Kelly didn't reply. She turned and walked quickly from the room. Her throat tightened and hot tears came to her eyes.

She drove back to town wondering where else to look for Steven. She had to find him now for his father's sake as well as her own. But how? She had exhausted all the possibilities long ago. What remained to be done?

As if from habit, her car turned off when she came to the road leading to the airport, and she parked in the lot adjacent to the Flyway Aviation building and went inside. The office was deserted, and she wandered around, reading the messages on the bulletin board, searching through the things on the desk, as if somehow a clue to Steven would leap into focus before her eyes.

Even if such a clue were available, it probably wouldn't be there. After all, this was Red's office and Red's desk. She had already asked him on her many visits to the hospital if he could help, but with no success. Red mentioned some places Steven might go, but none of the leads had turned up the man himself. Red's desk contained merely his own mail. Skewered to the spindle in the corner was a single sheet of paper, a list in Red's own handwriting, of jumps he planned to make now that he had returned to skydiving. Kelly sighed heavily as she scanned the list; it turned out to be a short-lived second career, she thought with dismay.

At last she left the airport and returned to her own office. Time wouldn't stand still while she attempted to solve the riddle of Steven's disappearance. A small mountain of work cluttered her desk, and she would have to wade though it today; it couldn't be put off any longer. She would tackle the search for Steven again tomorrow when she might feel better.

Most of her stack of mail went straight to the wastebasket. The nature of her job ensured that she would be on mailing lists for books, magazines, gift catalogues, and specialty advertising, and now the new opera promotion generated its own paperwork.

Amidst all of that, there were still reminders of the skydiving promotion, as she seemed to have gotten herself on every parachute club mailing list in just the few weeks she'd been involved. At first she wanted to hurl this

material into the round file too, and then decided that who-
ever took over the remaining events might need some of
the flyers, invitations, and information. She sorted through
it and made a neat pile on one corner of her desk. She'd
drop it off in Lyle's office before leaving.

Thinking of Lyle brought a flush to her cheeks again as
she remembered what he'd said at the banquet and how
she had forgiven him on the telephone the next day when
he called to apologize. She had purposely avoided him since
then—hence the work that had accumulated on her desk—
and she could only hope he wouldn't come in this afternoon. She didn't want to face him just now.

Hastily she sorted the myriad sheets of paper, giving a
thorough reading to the ones pertaining to the opera promotion, and at last she finished and could go home. She
rose wearily from the chair and stretched, arching her arms
high above her head to relieve the tension in her back. Then
she swung her head up and down slowly to stretch her
neck muscles. The pile of papers on skydiving came into
focus as she bent her head. "Morgan Hill," she read in
large flowery script, and underneath it, "James Air Field."

It triggered her memory: Morgan Hill had been the first
entry on the list she had seen on Red's desk only hours
ago. Then, halfway down the list of events, as if leaping
from the page, she read, "Red Johnson." Her heart lurched
at the sight of the name. He must have signed up for it
before the accident. She picked up the sheet of paper and
examined it more closely. The event would be held tomorrow, Saturday. But surely they knew he was in the hospital. Probably they hadn't had time to take his name off the
flyers before mailing them out.

She dropped the sheet on the desk and started to leave
the room. But what if they didn't know? She went back to

the desk, picking up the flyer once more. She saw no address or telephone number, merely the name of the parachute club. That was enough. She picked up the telephone and after twenty minutes and seven calls, she spoke to the man in charge of Saturday's event.

"You don't know me," Kelly began, "but I have a copy of your flyer about the meet at James Air Field tomorrow, and I happen to know that one of the skydivers, Red Johnson, will—"

"Red Johnson," the man on the other end of the line repeated. "Here's his application. He's new, I guess."

"Not really. He used to jump years ago. Anyway, the point is, he won't be jumping tomorrow. I thought you ought to know in case he hadn't informed you himself."

"No, he hadn't," the man answered. "In fact, I just talked to him the other day and he assured me he would be here."

Kelly's mouth dropped open and she couldn't find her voice for some seconds. "He called and said he would be there?"

"No, ma'am, he didn't call. He came here. I spoke to him in person."

"But that's impossible!" Kelly sputtered into the phone. "The man is in the hospital—"

"Are you sure we're talking about the same man, lady?"

"Yes, Red Johnson, a medium-sized man in his 60s, with red hair going gray. That's where he gets his name."

"Well, the Red Johnson I saw the other day is thirtyish, tall, and had dark curly hair. Come to think of it I should have asked how he came to be called 'Red'."

Kelly's heart almost stopped beating. It was Steven; it had to be! Why had he pretended to be Red? "Tell me," she said, "where can I reach this man? Do you have an address or phone?"

"Well, there's an address here somewhere." He rustled some papers. "Yeah, here it is. Flyway Aviation."

"I have that," Kelly said. "What about a telephone number?" But the number he gave her was the one in the Flyway office.

"Sorry, miss, but you can see him jump tomorrow."

"Yes, I guess I'll have to. Thanks for your help."

Fairly flying, Kelly raced from her office and down the hallway to the exit. She would drive to Morgan Hill at once and then to James Air Field.

But what if it wasn't Steven after all? It had to be, though; it just had to. Steven would do something like this, take Red's place. Her pounding heart told her it was true.

twelve

Kelly woke with a start, the sun warm on her face even through the curtains; she knew it was late, very late. Tossing the covers aside, she leaped from the bed and reached for her watch, discovering what she had suspected: it was almost nine o'clock.

All during her hurried shower and while pulling on her clothes, she berated herself for having trusted the motel office's wake-up call service. She should have known better, but what else could she have done?

When she'd gone to bed in the Moon Vista Inn the night before, she had thought nothing could keep her asleep past dawn, so that she could rush to the James Air Field before the activities started, find Steven, and give him the message from his father. But sleep had eluded her. After the swift packing, then driving all the way to Morgan Hill, with a short stop for dinner en route, she had registered at the motel, asked them to wake her at 7:30 this morning, and then tried to sleep. But she had tossed and turned for hours. Her active brain replayed the conversation she'd had with the man on the telephone, replayed her conversation with Mr. Trask about wanting to see his son, and, worst of all, had played, over and over, variations on the theme of what she would say to Steven when she finally saw him.

Then, as if to torment her more completely, she had relived the moments when she had been with Steven, his strong arms around her. She had flopped onto her stomach, pulling the pillow over her head, as if this would shut out the scenes, but then she turned again, flung the hot blankets away and brushed her hair from her face, praying that Steven would be there, and hoping for sleep to spirit her away into unconsciousness.

When sleep had finally come, it had taken a drug-like form, with the result that she had slept too soundly; her usual rising hour had come and gone without her knowledge.

She drove as fast as she dared, eyes constantly scanning the sides of the highway, watching for signs that would take her to the air field. At last it came into sight, and the many cars already parked in the gravel-covered lot told her she was dreadfully late.

She told herself she could just as easily find Steven after the events—that if he intended to jump in Red's place, he wasn't going anywhere until he'd done that—and she could talk to him then. Yet fears he might leave the area somehow without her knowledge refused to leave. She paid her entrance fee at the gate and walked boldly toward the hangar, hoping to look as if she knew her way around so no one would stop her.

Inside, everyone looked alike, as usual all dressed in jumpsuits and helmets, fastening on two parachutes. She looked for the tallest man, but some were hunched over equipment, others were seated tying on their boots, and she had to circle the room before she spotted Steven, her heart leaping into her throat. He saw her at the same moment, and his eyes first widened in surprise, then narrowed, as if he had no wish to see her there.

She approached him timidly, all the rehearsed speeches from the night before forgotten as she stared into his familiar face. She longed to stretch on her tiptoes and plant a kiss on that mouth, remembering how it had claimed hers in the past.

Wrenching her thoughts to the present, she said, "Steven, I have to talk to you."

"I haven't time," he answered tersely. "How did you find me, anyway?"

"I saw Red's name on a flyer for this exhibition and when I called they said he would jump today. I knew—that is, I suspected—you came to take his place."

Steven glanced away from her, buckling his harness more tightly, and muttered, "Regular little detective, aren't you?"

Kelly blanched at the hardness of his tone. In her heart she'd hoped he'd be overjoyed to see her, but that was unrealistic of course, at least until she could explain. "I had to find you, not just for myself, but—"

"I don't expect you to understand," he interrupted, his tone softening somewhat, "but I had to do this."

"But I do understand," Kelly said. "I know how much you care for Red."

He frowned again. "That had nothing to do with it. I wanted to jump and I couldn't do it under my own name. This seemed an ideal way. Besides," he added, "after all these years I can't just quit skydiving overnight. You don't know what it's like. Once you've been up there, you just have to. . ."

"It's true I haven't jumped," she said, "and I guess I don't understand the attraction. But I'm also sure that's not your entire reason. You'd rather die than let anyone think you have altruistic thoughts, but I remember all you told me that night after Red's accident. You were trying to protect Red's name, to make a jump that would go down in the books as his, weren't you?"

He didn't answer, only turned and left the hangar.

Kelly hurried after him, clutching the sleeve of his white jumpsuit. "Steven, wait, I haven't told you why I came. It's terribly important."

"I don't think we have anything important to say to one another anymore," he said, but his eyes raked her face as if trying to impress on his memory every curve and line of it.

"But we do," she insisted, now running to keep up with his long strides across the field. "It's your father."

He stopped suddenly, forcing her to do the same, and they looked at each other. "What about my father?"

"He wants you. He asked me to find you. He needs an operation, and he doesn't want to have it without seeing you first. He wants to make peace with you in case he. . ."

Steven's head turned, and he watched the others, now far from him, boarding helicopters that would take them aloft. "I have to go. I'll be back soon." He struck off again.

Suddenly Kelly felt as if she would never see him again if she let him leave her now. She ran behind, gasping out words. "There's more. I'm not engaged to my boss; I never was. He had no right to say what he did. I would have explained it to you that night, but you never gave me a chance."

Again he stopped and looked at her. Then he said, "Come with me."

Kelly nodded, knowing that nothing mattered but being with him. He took her hand and pulled her along, and they approached one of the helicopters. Instinctively they ducked their heads out of the danger of the turning rotor blades and ran toward the open doorway. He boosted her up, and she found herself in a large empty space behind the single pilot. Shouting over the incredibly loud noise, she tried to make herself heard. "What shall I do?"

"First put this on." He pulled a parachute from the storage space under the wooden seat.

Perspiration forming beads on her forehead, hands fumbling with nervousness, she opened the harness and stepped into it. Steven put his hands around her waist, helping her, and she wanted to melt in his arms.

But he pulled away from her and said gruffly, "These birds aren't like airplanes; you can't glide them down. If anything happens, they drop like a rock. Nobody ought to get into one without a parachute."

As if that were a signal, the noise increased in tone and pitch, and the helicopter rose from its pad, Kelly watching through the open door as the ground fell away. She backed up and sat on the rough seat, Steven seating himself beside her.

"I only have a few minutes," he said. "Tell me exactly what my father said."

"He told me the doctors insist on an immediate operation."

"Is it serious?"

"Yes, but not necessarily fatal. They wouldn't have suggested the operation if they didn't think—"

"Doctor's don't know everything! Look at Red!"

"Your father will be all right," Kelly said, putting her hand over his. "But he wants to see you first. He wants to tell you he forgives you—and to ask you to forgive him for all these years. He said he wished he had done it years ago. He admitted he'd been a stubborn old man."

"Stubborn?" Steven repeated, flinging the word out and raising his eyes upward. "I'm the stubborn one. And a fool!"

"No," Kelly said. "You mustn't blame yourself too much." She wished she could say more, but having to shout her words over the din of the engine made it too difficult.

"It's really funny," Steven said. "Do you know that I planned to see him tomorrow anyway?"

"You did?"

"He hasn't been out of my thoughts for two minutes ever since I left you that night. Finally I decided I had to go back and see him, beg for his forgiveness, make it up to him somehow. And now I find out he wants to see me too."

He got to his feet, pulling on gloves, but his face showed some confusion. "Did you mean what you said about not marrying your boss? You're not in love with him?"

Kelly got up and leaned close to him. "Yes, I meant it. I was never in love with him. I've never loved anyone but you."

He pulled her to him and crushed her against the reserve parachute strapped to his chest. "I've loved you since the first time I saw you in a jumpsuit. I want to marry you, Kelly." He kissed her fiercely, holding her so tightly she thought her breathing would stop.

When his lips finally left hers, he looked adoringly at her again. "I've been such a fool, but I'll try not to be anymore. I've learned some new things lately. That's what I went to San Francisco that night to tell you. I've given my life to Christ at last."

The pilot turned and yelled at them. "Will you please jump?"

"Oh, Steven, I can't let you go now. Let me jump with you."

He stared at her. "What are you saying? You were always afraid to jump."

"I don't want to be without you. I'm not afraid anymore. Now that I know we both belong to God, I can do anything!"

The pilot yelled again. Making up his mind in an instant, Steven quickly removed his helmet. "Here," he said, putting it on Kelly's head. "You need this more than I do." After he strapped it beneath her chin, he leaned forward and kissed her again. "Do you remember everything?"

"Yes," she breathed, her ecstacy over knowing they loved one another completely obliterating even a hint of fear for doing what she had once vowed she'd never attempt. "I remember all the ground training. I can do it!"

"I'm going to be with you almost every second," he said. "We're going together. I'll hold your hand, and I'll stay with you until you open your chute. I'll free-fall farther and then open mine lower down so that I'll land first. Then I can be on the ground before you and catch you."

"I know how to fall," Kelly said, her voice sounding strange through the helmet covering her ears. "You taught me, you know."

He laughed, then took a firm grip on her hand and led her to the open doorway. He looked down and got his bearings on the field below. His free hand on the doorway, he stepped onto the landing skids of the helicopter, then tugged gently on Kelly's arms, urging her to do the same.

The moment she stepped out, the wind seemed to whip at her clothes, filling her with an icy chill. But the incredible beauty of the azure sky, with no clouds anywhere in sight, the ground beneath checkered into patches of greens, browns, and golds, claimed her attention. Then Steven's gaze caught hers again and he nodded his head. "Now," he shouted.

They leaped into space together, and as if she had been doing it all her life, Kelly arched her body and stretched out her arms and legs in the stable position. She thought her heart would burst from her chest with exhilaration.

She was flying!

There was no sound, no sensation of falling, only the faint hiss of air past her helmet and the tug of wind against her slacks and sleeves. She felt free as a bird, soaring through the silken sky like a butterfly. She wanted to sing, but her breath seemed to be trapped, and she could utter no sound.

The experience was like no other in her entire life. No wonder skydivers loved the sport. No wonder they delayed opening their parachutes as long as possible, never wanting to end that spectacular moment when they felt exempt from the laws of gravity and floated to earth like beings from another planet.

She looked at Steven and found his eyes searching hers, lips smiling. She grinned at him in return, wishing she could say all the things that were racing through her mind, yet knowing that he understood. He, of all people, understood.

All too soon he signalled for her to pull her rip cord. Was the ground really that close? It didn't seem to be coming up rapidly at all; she didn't want the moment to end. Dutifully, however, she grasped the metal handle, and when he nodded to her, she pulled it. But nothing happened and she looked at Steven in surprise. The ring came away in her hands, little wires attached to it, but she continued to float. Then, suddenly, she was snatched upward and out of Steven's handclasp. She felt as if her arms were being torn out of their sockets.

She looked at the canopy above, plain white and round, with no directional gores—not a sport parachute—but at this moment, perfect. None of the things that could go wrong had occurred; she almost felt cheated of the opportunity to practice what she had learned about emergencies. But then she remembered Steven had told her they were a "once-in-a-lifetime" possibility.

She grasped the lines and looked down. Steven was doing somersaults and backloops. Finally his parachute began to deploy, and he disappeared beneath its brightly striped canopy. What an odd sensation, seeing a parachute below you instead of above!

The ground came up at her at increasingly faster speeds. The patches gave way to one large brown area, the drop zone, and now she had to remember how to land, how to fall and roll so as not to injure herself, just the way she had practiced it.

But there was no need to worry about doing it properly today; Steven stood beneath her, and with a thud, she crashed into him. They went tumbling over and over in the dirt, tangled in the parachutes, laughing and kissing all at once.

❧

The next week they sat on one of the many sofas in the waiting room of the hospital, holding hands and whispering their love for one another, a decided contrast from the moment when they had shouted their love over the noise of a helicopter in flight.

"I can hardly believe what's happened," she said.

"That I'm a real Christian at last? I wasn't ready before, but you helped me find my way back to Christ. That's why I went to Pastor Wallace."

"But what did you do before that, all those long weeks when I was so worried about you?" She searched his face with adoring eyes and held his hand in a tight grip.

"I went to a little cabin in the mountains. I think I knew a long time ago that I'd have to find God again, but I still kept fighting it. You see, I'd never forgiven Him for taking my mother away from me."

"But He didn't." She squeezed his hand for emphasis.

"I know that now. But when Red had the accident, I just resisted all the more. Now I know better."

She rested her head on his shoulder. "I'm so happy for you, for both of us."

"I feel like a new person. I'm truly born again, Kelly. I made my peace over my mother and Red, and then I came to tell you."

"And Lyle spoiled everything."

"It was a test and I almost failed. But then I knew that even if I lost you, I could never lose God again. That was why I was going to see my father, to ask his forgiveness."

"I'm so glad, Steven."

A doctor appeared in the doorway and informed them that Mr. Trask was now awake and ready to see them. "He's still very weak," he warned. "The anesthetic made him nauseous for awhile, but he's feeling better now and anxious to see you. As I told you earlier, the operation was a total success."

Still holding hands, Steven and Kelly ascended in the elevator to the fifth floor and walked the cool clean corridor until they found the right room. There, looking like a tiny frail figure in the stark white bed, lay Steven's father. He heard their footsteps, and his blue eyes flashed in their direction. Then his thin pale face broke into a smile.

"Come here," he said, raising his hands toward them.

"Now, don't overdo," Steven admonished, rushing forward and taking his father's hands into his own large strong ones.

"I'm fine now," the old man said, his gaze traveling back and forth between the two young people in front of him. "The doctor says I'll be up and around in no time at all. Pretty good, eh?" He chuckled. Then he coughed, and he dropped his head back down on the pillow and closed his eyes.

"Take it easy," Steven remonstrated. "Yes, you're going to be fine, but just rest until you get your strength back."

The man's eyes opened again, and he again smiled at them, but otherwise remained still in the bed. After a pause, he said softly, "I can't tell you how happy I am. I have you back, Steven, I'm to have this beautiful golden child for my daughter-in-law, and now the operation is over and I'll have many years left to enjoy what God has so graciously given me."

"I only wish I hadn't been so stupid for so long," Steven said.

"No, no," his father said. "Don't say that. There's no need for regrets. I have enough of them of my own, but we won't speak of them anymore. This is a time for rejoicing and for planning. Now that I know I can do it, I want to be part of the wedding. We'll have a big church wedding—"

"Wait a minute," Steven said, "perhaps Kelly has some other ideas. It's her wedding too, you know."

"I haven't even thought that far ahead," she answered. "My mother's coming up next week to meet you and Steven, and we can all talk about it then. But you must get well first."

"Yes," Steven agreed. "You know how impatient I am. I can't wait forever to marry this lovely daredevil here. I'm only human."

They all laughed, remembering Kelly's first, and so far only, parachute jump. Then Mr. Trask turned serious eyes on them again. "I promise to get well if you promise not to do any more jumping out of airplanes until after the wedding. After that, I know you'll both be at it again."

"But only as a hobby," Steven reminded him.

"So, instead of one skydiver in the family, I shall have two. Or maybe more?" he added.

Kelly saw the doctor enter the room. "I think we're being asked to leave you to your rest now," she said. She and Steven each kissed his father on the cheek, and then, arms around one another, they left the hospital.

As they paused on the broad steps of the building, facing green lawns and neatly clipped hedges, Kelly asked, "Did you mean that? About only skydiving as a hobby?"

"Yes. I can't give it up completely, but I'm ready to take up my responsibilities to my father's company now."

"Will you miss it terribly?"

"The constant round of teaching, flying, jumping? No, not really. To tell the truth, I began to be dissatisfied with my life a long while before all this happened. I think Red guessed. But after I met you, I knew I was being led in this direction, back to being a Trask again."

"Well, I hope you won't mind if I make a few jumps," Kelly said. "I hate to eat humble pie, but I must retract everything I ever said about it being a stupid sport. I know I'll never look up at the sky again without remembering how it feels to fly through it."

Steven took her into his arms. "I have you now and that's just as exciting to me. I'm going to spend the rest of my life making you happy."

"Oh, Steven," Kelly whispered, but her words were smothered by his lips on hers. She held him tightly, forgetting all sense of time and place in the joy of their love. She felt part of an entire universe filled with God's love, and it was like. . .yes, like free-falling through an immense heaven of boundless blue sky.

A Letter To Our Readers

Dear Reader:

In order that we might better contribute to your reading enjoyment, we would appreciate your taking a few minutes to respond to the following questions. When completed, please return to the following:

Rebecca Germany, Editor
Heartsong Presents
P.O. Box 719
Uhrichsville, Ohio 44683

1. Did you enjoy reading *Flying High*?
   - ❏ Very much. I would like to see more books by this author!
   - ❏ Moderately
     I would have enjoyed it more if _____
     _____

2. Are you a member of **Heartsong Presents**? ❏Yes ❏No
   If no, where did you purchase this book? _____
   _____

3. What influenced your decision to purchase this book? (Check those that apply.)

❏ Cover	❏ Back cover copy
❏ Title	❏ Friends
❏ Publicity	❏ Other_____

4. How would you rate, on a scale from 1 (poor) to 5 (superior), **Heartsong Presents'** new cover design?_____

5. On a scale from 1 (poor) to 10 (superior), please rate
   the following elements.

   ___Heroine   ___Plot

   ___Hero   ___Inspirational theme

   ___Setting   ___Secondary characters

6. What settings would you like to see covered in
   Heartsong Presents books?_____

   _____

   _____

7. What are some inspirational themes you would like
   to see treated in future books?_____

   _____

   _____

8. Would you be interested in reading other **Heartsong
   Presents** titles?   ❏ Yes   ❏ No

9. Please check your age range:
   ❏ Under 18   ❏ 18-24   ❏ 25-34
   ❏ 35-45   ❏ 46-55   ❏ Over 55

10. How many hours per week do you read? _____

Name _____

Occupation_____

Address_____

City_____ State_____ Zip _____

Introducing New Authors!

___**Rae Simons**—*The Quiet Heart*—Thrilled at the opportunity to work near Liam, the love of her life, Dorrie has accepted a teaching position in a school for troubled children. Dorrie is desperate to please Liam and be the person he thinks she is. Will Dorrie ever possess a quiet heart? HP114 $2.95

___ **Birdie L. Etchison**—*The Heart Has Its Reasons*—Emily, the simple Quaker, wants only a simple life. But things get complicated when her dashing friend introduces her to handsome Ben Galloway. As she sorts through her conflicting emotions, Emily finds that love and committment are anything but simple decisions. HP123 $2.95

___**Mary LaPietra**—*His Name on Her Heart*—Marnette is haunted by her past. As God's plan unfolds, Marnette finds herself living with previously unknown relatives in the newly settled prairie. Although she constructs a tissue of lies about her past, Marnette is not as successful in denying her attraction to Drew Britton. HP124 $2.95

___**Elizabeth Murphey**—*Love's Tender Gift*—Determined to prove herself to Joel, Val decides to infiltrate a local cult as a class project. But she isn't prepared for her own vulnerability to the persuasive tactics of the cult. With Val's life in danger, Joel follows her to Ireland where she has been lured by promises of eternal life and love. Will Joel find Val in time to convince her that she already has his love...and God's? HP125 $2.95

·····Hearts♥ng·····

·········· Presents ··········

Great Inspirational Romance at a Great Price!

Heartsong Presents books are inspirational romances in contemporary and historical settings, designed to give you an enjoyable, spirit-lifting reading experience. You can choose from 144 wonderfully written titles from some of today's best authors like Colleen L. Reece, Brenda Bancroft, Janelle Jamison, and many others.

When ordering quantities less than twelve, above titles are $2.95 each.

Hearts♥ng Presents
Love Stories Are Rated G!

That's for godly, gratifying, and of course, great! If you love a thrilling love story, but don't appreciate the sordidness of popular paperback romances, **Heartsong Presents** is for you. In fact, **Heartsong Presents** is the *only inspirational romance book club*, the only one featuring love stories where Christian faith is the primary ingredient in a marriage relationship.

Sign up today to receive your first set of four, never before published Christian romances. Send no money now; you will receive a bill with the first shipment. You may cancel at any time without obligation, and if you aren't completely satisfied with any selection, you may return the books for an immediate refund!

Imagine. . .four new romances every four weeks—two historical, two contemporary—with men and women like you who long to meet the one God has chosen as the love of their lives. . .all for the low price of $9.97 postpaid.

To join, simply complete the coupon below and mail to the address provided. **Heartsong Presents** romances are rated G for another reason: They'll arrive *Godspeed!*